Death & the Detective

AN ARCANA GLEN SWEET PARANORMAL ROMANCE

TAROT FANTASY MAJOR ARCANA SERIES
BOOK SEVEN

TARA MAYA

Misque Press

Welcome to Arcana Glen, a magical town hidden in the Rocky Mountains of Colorado....

Here arcanes of all types are free to be themselves... Elves, Witches, Shifters, Seraphs, Dragons and more.

But until the Twenty-Two Guardians are restored to power, the Elven War rages among the arcanes. What's the solution?

True Love, of course!

To read a free love story and sneak a peek at what happened before the Massacre of the Guardians, ten years ago, CLICK HERE to sign up for the newsletter for Tara's Tribe and receive the free novella, ***The Genie & the Gymnast.***

About This Book

Miles Malone died last night.

No one is more surprised than he is when he crawls out of a dumpster this morning, the blast hole in his chest magically healed.

Weird.

He doesn't believe in magic, though he has no other explanation. The Magician might have more information, but he'll only share if Miles agrees to do something for him in return... but Miles doesn't trust the eccentric billionaire who **seems to think magic is real.**

Meanwhile, Miles has a job to do. He's a private investigator, and a woman has come to him figure out the mystery of why healthy young men are dying at a local veteran's hospital.

Miles is afraid it might have something to do with **the beautiful woman he invited on a date** for the Fourth of July picnic. A nurse that patients call **the Angel of Death...**

Welcome to Arcana Glen, a magical town hidden in the Rocky Mountains of Colorado....

Here arcanes of all types are free to be themselves... Elves, Witches, Shifters, Seraphs, Dragons and more.

But until the Twenty-Two Guardians are restored to power, the Elven War rages among the arcanes. What's the solution?

True Love, of course!

One

June 16, 2022
Thursday, 07:56 am

THE FIRST THING he noticed was the stench. It smelled like the inside of a dumpster.

The second thing he noticed was that he was inside of a dumpster.

It was dark and cramped, but the top metal lid was open just enough that the early morning grey light revealed the silhouettes of various hunks of trash that covered his body.

Miles Malone had woken up with some weird hangovers in some weird places and next to some sketchy people before. But this was the worst. His chest hurt. He wondered if he had been punched, knocked unconscious and dumped in the trash by his assailant. He hoped it was at least multiple assailants, but he had a vague memory of getting surprised by a big guy...

The big guy couldn't have possibly thrown a fireball at me? Nah, c'mon.

Obviously, his memory of events was still foggy. First things first. Miles concentrated on climbing out of the dumpster. His chest twinged in pain with every move he made. He finally straddled the rim and was about to complete his jump to the pavement below when a cop car pulled into the parking space in front of the dumpster. It was from the local sheriff's department. The town of Arcana Glen was a somewhat remote mountain hamlet. It needed enough of a police force to keep criminals from harassing rich tourists who came to ski in the winter and water ski in the summer. But there wasn't a lot of crime otherwise.

Miles had grown up in Denver. He'd joined the police force there before he'd suffered a near-death experience at work, followed by a divorce. Bitter and wearied, he decided to try the slower lane in a mountain town. He was still getting used to feeling like a stranger in a tightknit community. He had made the effort to get to know the local police, but they were very cool towards him. He understood that he had to work with the sheriff's department. However, just when he'd been making some headway befriending the sheriff, Sheriff Spencer Lawson was involved in a messy scandal. His younger brother, Cody Lawson, took over. Miles didn't know if he could trust Cody, and the feeling was mutual.

Cody Lawson sauntered over to where Miles was stuck half-way out of the dumpster. Cody tipped his hat up on his forehead as he pierced Miles with a *"what the hell are you up-to, asshole?"* expression.

"Hey, Cody." Miles didn't wave, but he tried to sound casual as he lowered himself out of the dumpster.

"You okay there, Malone?" asked Cody, giving him a suspicious once-over.

"Sure. Why wouldn't I be?" Miles dusted the remains of a burrito off his shirt. Man, that was going to leave a stain.

Of the two brothers, Miles considered Cody to be the more aggressive one, and the least friendly. In fact, Cody had tried to warn Miles off of staying in the town when Miles first arrived. Specifically, Cody had told him, "Someone like you won't do well in a place like this. Arcana Glen is not the relaxing mountain retreat you're expecting. A lot of strange things happen here."

Cody had never clarified what he meant. For a while Miles wondered if everyone in town belonged to the same cult, since an awful lot of the residents attended the same church run by a suspicious character named Pastor Mike. Pastor Mike was so squeaky clean, he had to be hiding something, in Miles' opinion. But despite his distrust of clergy, Miles had to admit not everybody belonged to that church, and eventually he eventually dismissed the cult theory. Finally, he concluded it was just the typical 'small-town vs outsiders' vibe. The residents of Arcana Glen seemed to think they had some special knowledge about the universe which other people weren't entitled to share. Miles really hated that kind of attitude. Not that he was willing to share secrets of his own when he got a hold of them. He just couldn't stand for anyone else to have something secret *from him*.

Cody's warning, whether kindly or maliciously meant, had the opposite effect on Miles. It made him determined to put down roots in the town come hell or high water. He told his real estate agent, Pamela Newton, that he had decided to buy rather than lease. That was how he acquired his current residence, a work/home townhouse that also served as his office. He had a bedroom and kitchen for himself upstairs, an office and reception area for himself and his secretary downstairs.

"I got reports of a body in the dumpster," said Cody. He was still giving Miles the dirty eye.

"Well," said Miles cheerfully. "I can tell you: I was just inside the dumpster, and I didn't see a body."

Cody cleared his throat. "I think you *were* the body, Miles."

"What? Me? Well, in that case you can go home. Look at me. I'm fine. As a matter of fact, just the other day, I was looking at burial plots and I thought, 'that's the last thing I need.'"

"Were you really...?" Cody looked alarmed.

"It's a joke, Lawson. Besides, when I go, I don't want to be buried. I want to be cremated. It's my only chance to have a smokin' hot body."

"Malone..." Cody shook his head. "You have a big-ass hole in the middle of your chest. Like your heart and lungs were burnt out. I'm not really sure how you're walking around, never mind talking. You need to go to a hospital in Denver."

Miles glanced down at his chest and saw that Cody was correct. His chest had been hollowed out by a huge gaping burn, exposing seared muscles and burnt ribs.

Privately, Miles freaked out a little bit.

No, he could not explain the hole. However, as he stared at it, the flesh of his chest seemed to surge forward and knit itself back together. The shirt did not. The burnt edges still hung loosely from his sore shoulders. His pecs and abs, however, now looked smooth, and, he was pleased to see, showed evidence that his daily jogs in the woods, where he took advantage of the free exercise equipment placed at intervals along the nature trail had him beginning to look like a gym rat instead of a city rat.

"What hole?" he asked Cody. Miles rubbed his healed chest.

There were a lot of ways Miles anticipated Cody might react. Cody might stammer and shout in disbelief. He might rub his eyes and mutter, "I must've imagined it." He might freak out and arrest Miles for being some kind of ghoulish zombie. But Miles never anticipated what Cody actually said.

Cody picked up his walkie-talkie. "We've got a Code Platinum."

Then Cody waved at Miles with a weird little smile. "I have a feeling I'll be seeing you around, Miles. Take care of yourself and try not to ruin any more shirts."

Small towns are weird, Miles thought. *Maybe Cody Lawson was right. This one is weirder than most.*

❧

June 16,
Thursday, 08:09

The dumpster happened to be right up against the back of Miles' own building. He jogged around to the front so he wouldn't startle his secretary, Eva White, by climbing in through the fire escape. It was just past eight o'clock on a Thursday morning, so she was already there preparing coffee for both of them. Eva had twinkling eyes, smooth dark skin, a generous girth, and an unflappable, if slightly edgy, sense of humor.

"There you are," she said. "Honeycakes, you're all kinds of sexy, but I'm married. You better put on a shirt that hasn't been wrapped around a grenade."

"Oh...yeah. Sorry, Eva. I keep extra clothes in the office, I'll change."

"Girl trouble or goon trouble?" she asked.

"A little of both." He shrugged out of his shirt. The more he remembered about what had happened yesterday evening, the less sense it made. "I think."

"I've got your favorite kind of mail." She brandished some letters like a Viking mace.

"Invitations to dine at the Castle?" he joked.

"Bills," she replied tartly. "Also, you haven't paid me for last month. My new washing machine ain't going to pay for itself."

"Uh oh, sounds like I'm in *loads* of trouble!"

"Get out of here with your jokes!" She pretended to be mad but couldn't suppress her smile.

"I'm trying to think of a *dirty* laundry joke to tell, but they all come out *clean*."

"Give me my money, or I'm gonna return that machine and make *you* come to my house and wash my dishes." She snorted, returning to her desk. "Invitation to the Castle, my ass."

The Castle was a huge building that had been designed at the end of the 19th century to look like a fairytale medieval castle. It was the residence of the Magician. The Magician was a stage show performer who had started in Las Vegas, and through merchandising his own brand and prudent investments in real estate, for instance here in Arcana Glen, but also elsewhere across the country, had turned a side show circus act into a billion-dollar corporation. He was so reclusive almost no one saw him in person, yet his personality dominated the town in the same way the absurd Castle dominated the view from Main Street. Miles was thinking of him right now because of what Sheriff Cody Lawson had said.

Miles knew all the police codes and he never heard of Code Platinum. And who had the Sheriff called? The police station, or someone else... like Alephander Guiscard, the Magician? Miles had never heard of the local police force answering to a Las Vegas entertainer before, but in this town.... *Rich people*, he thought in disgust. *The guy probably owns the whole police department, along with the rest of the town.*

Miles accepted a cup of joe and ambled into his office. First, he tossed the burnt shirt in the overflowing trash can and grabbed a new one from the top drawer of his file cabinet. Next, he pulled out an envelope from the case he had worked on over the weekend, the same case that had turned nasty at the end of last night and somehow resulted in him climbing out of a dumpster this morning. He was still hazy on the details, but he distinctly remembered his sketchy client, Owen McGee, handing him an envelope filled with crisp hundred-dollar bills at the start of the case, back on June 8. Miles went back into the front office and handed the whole thing to Eva White.

"Here's your pay for this month and last month as well," he said proudly. "Now you can buy your washing machine. I hope that takes *a load* off your mind."

Eva rolled her eyes. "You gonna kill me with your terrible puns one day."

"Laundry puns aren't so bad. They just get *a bad press.*"

Eva waved a fist at him. Miles chuckled. Now he just had to figure out how to cover the mortgage. If he could get another gig, one that paid as well as the last one he had taken, although preferably without the dumpster....

Eva opened the envelope. "Well, honey, you're lucky I know you well enough to realize you like pranks. This ain't money."

She dumped the envelope out on her desk. Little toy play bills, the kind an impatient mom would buy in a supermarket at the checkout stand to placate a crying kid, spilled all over the desk. The toy bills had cartoon faces instead of dead presidents, and the label "100 Lucky Doolers!" was printed in bubble letters. There were exactly the correct number pretend bills as Miles had negotiated with his client, but Miles couldn't understand how he had missed the fact they were fake. They weren't even green. They were rainbow striped bills. Rainbow!

"That swindling bastard," swore Miles. "I swear I saw the real bills, Eva. I don't know how he switched them out."

A thought occurred to Miles. It could've happened anytime overnight when he was unconscious in the dumpster. Probably, he should be glad nothing worse had happened to him than getting swindled. But this put him in an awkward position.

Apparently, Cody Lawson had been correct. It was more difficult than Miles thought to drum up business in a town like Arcana Glen. He had trouble even getting the usual cases he expected to be covering as a P.I., divorce and adultery cases, for instance.

Look at the latest case. Owen McGee and Eleni Bendox arrived together. Owen McGee, the swindler who had cheated Miles out of his money, asked Miles to investigate who tried to kill Eleni Bendox. Miles found the evidence but couldn't reach either client. Then Bendox called Miles and warned him not to trust McGee. She wanted to meet with Miles alone, but McGee showed up, harassing her, warning her not to speak to Miles. Trying to be her knight in shining armor, Miles stepped in front of her to protect her from McGee.

Then... something like a giant hawk attacked out of the sky.

Okay, this was the point where things got fuzzy. What Miles remembered was seeing something like a Dark Angel fly from the sky, land in front of him, and blast him in the chest with a ball of fire.

Maybe it was the Angel of Death, Miles speculated.

But more likely, it was a hallucination he experienced after a perfectly boring death, getting shot by Owen McGee. Miles almost died... obviously, he hadn't died, or he couldn't have crawled out of the dumpster... and hallucinated about black-winged angels.

That made more sense.

McGee had shot him in the chest.

Shot him? Or burned him? Surely the guy had not ejected a baseball-sized sphere of flame from the palm of his hand. And surely the guy had not had huge wings like bat wings but made out of pure shadow...

And yet that image was burned into Miles' memory the same way that a giant, oozing hole had been burned into his chest.

No! None of that makes sense! Miles shook his head. *Stick to the facts.* Whatever he imagined he'd seen right before he was knocked unconscious could be attributed to the trauma.

"I'm sorry, Eva. I'm going to pay you."

"Don't forget you have to pay the mortgage on this place as well," she said.

"I know, I know..."

He returned to his office.

A few moments later, Eva came in. She wore a big smile plastered across her face. "Guess what? Looks like your invitation to the Castle came in after all. This letter is hot!"

Usually *hot* meant *urgent*, but when Miles accepted the envelope, he dropped it on his desk. It was surrounded by a nimbus of light and warm to touch, though the envelope did not actually burn him. The sender's address was written as: **Alephander Guiscard, The Magician, Arcana Castle, Arcana Glen, Colorado**, and included the ZIP Code.

Miles tore open the letter. It was stamped with a date at the top, today's date, and a time, which he realized was about the time he had climbed out of the dumpster. What the hell? Could the Magician have known that something strange happened? Miles recalled Cody reporting, "Code Platinum," to someone. Had the police reported Miles odd recovery to Alephander Guiscard? And again, why would the police do that? Why would Guiscard care about Miles's dumpster diving habit?

The letter read simply:

Mr. Malone,
    I have a job for you. More details when you apply.
    Yours truly, A.
    PS find a date. You cannot be single.

What. The. Actual. F....

If it had just been a request for a job, no matter how mysterious, Miles innate curiosity would have overcome his equally instinctive sense of self-preservation. He'd done a few jobs for Guiscard before and applied for a few that he hadn't been awarded. Guiscard always paid well on the jobs that Miles did get.

Miles would have accepted the mystery invite, just to see what it was about. But the addendum that he needed to find a date and "could not be single" struck Miles as a whole level of creepy he was not willing to explore. Especially considering the rumors about Guiscard's love life. Supposedly Alephander Guiscard had gone through a long string of wives, most of whom disappeared under mysterious circumstances. He had just remarried for the seventh time in a secret ceremony in January. A second ceremony had been held, open to the public, in February. The guy was definitely a few marbles short of a jacks set. Miles had no intention of bringing any woman within sight of him.

Miles went to the window of his townhouse. French doors opened onto a small balcony that overlooked the street. He usually enjoyed sitting there after his morning jog—especially since every morning at the same time he was sitting there drinking his coffee, a very beautiful woman passed by on her white bicycle. One of these days he would get up the nerve to ask her what her name was and where she was headed every morning. For now, all he could do was wave as she waved back.

Right now, though, he wanted to see if any men were suspiciously lingering in the street, or if any cars were parked for no reason nearby. This letter had not come through the regular mail, despite the stamp in the corner.

Miles didn't smoke but he always carried a lighter. He took it out now, placed the letter on the cement of his balcony and burned it. The glow around the letter disappeared first and when the black wrinkly paper died down, he stomped out the remainder of the embers with his foot. Then he swept the ashes and threw them away. He didn't see anyone outside, but he had the feeling of being watched.

"That's my answer!" Miles Malone shouted out to whoever was spying on him. "Hope you don't need a crystal ball to figure out what that means!"

Two

June 16, 2022
08:59

MERCY WISE CLIMBED off her bicycle and chained it to the bicycle rack. She didn't own a car, but in a town like Arcana Glen, you hardly needed a car to get around town. She preferred the exercise. She knew she didn't look athletic to outsiders. She was short, 5'3", with a round baby face, plump although feminine curves, and thighs that did not have any sky between them. She knew she didn't exactly look like a warrior demigoddess, unless the field of battle was her kitchen table, and the enemy was a vicious tub of cookie dough ice cream. But was it her fault that she was big boned? Her human size was much shorter than what her arcane soul expected her to be. It was a common problem with shape shifters. Her body wanted to devour the amount of calories her arcane half needed, but her human half had to pay the price.

Mercy sighed. Just one more reason she would probably never find a man. The men who were attracted to her in her humble human form wanted someone soft, round, sweet, meek, and cuddly. Which, most of the time, she totally was. But then they saw her other form, and they ran screaming in the other direction.

Men who first met her in her arcane form, however, were even worse. They loved the dangerous Death Goddess appeal of her special brand of reaper. But when they met her as a human, they were disappointed. The worst was the reaper she had dated a few years ago: Yorgath the Undying Scourge. He was not the same kind of reaper as she, but "reaper adjacent," as her parents like to say; her parents had arranged the match.

"We're not going to arrange your marriage, we just want to introduce you to some suitable boys," her mother had explained. The next thing Mercy knew, Yorgath came over for dinner when Mercy and her family were all wearing their full arcane glory, and Yorgath had been totally smitten.

Everything went great that night. But the next week, he agreed to take her out for dinner and a movie in downtown Arcana Glen. Since they were going to be on Main Street, among mundanes, they both went human. He looked gorgeous as a human man. In fact, Mercy preferred that form of his to his reaper persona: a 9' skeleton in a bloody clown suit. But the minute Yorgath saw Mercy, the clown was the one who doubled over laughing.

"That's what you look like as a human?" he repeated over and over. "I can't believe you're really a…"

That's when she slapped him. Of course, since she was human at the time, it didn't hurt him one tiny bit. It didn't even stop him from laughing. She ended the date there and then, and stomped home to tell her parents no more blind dates. She hadn't even gotten dinner out of it, dang it.

As soon as Mercy entered the automatic double doors of the Arcana Glen Veteran's Hospital where she worked as an RN, another Nurse, Beverly Howard, ran up to her. Beverly was a mundane. Honestly, Mercy couldn't understand why the hospital hired Beverly to work at an institution that secretly catered to arcane veterans, including a lot of dangerous animal Shifters. Lots of Shifters were attracted to the military, but when they became older or sick, they were afraid to seek medical assistance for fear of being misunderstood. It was not so much a fear of exposure, because most mundanes would refuse to believe in magic no matter what, but the possibility of not getting adequate medical care was a very real danger.

About 20% of the human population were "sensitives," aware of magic and able to remember it existed, although they had none of their own. For some reason, it seemed to Mercy that this small group included the best, but also the worst, of humanity. The bad ones were those who took advantage of the ignorance of their fellow humans to hunt down the arcanes for their own corrupt purposes. Mercy did not mind mundanes, but she was leery of sensitives.

"Oh, thank goodness you're here," Beverly said clutching her chest, clearly flustered. "There's a bear! A bear in Mr Burnhard's room. I've called animal control... But you know how they are. They don't take these things seriously. There is a dangerous animal! What is animal control there for if they don't take care of something like that? Do you know what they asked me? They asked me how old I thought the bear was! How am I supposed to know the age of a bear?"

"I'll take care of it," Mercy said.

"Mercy, no, you can't go in there..." Beverly's voice trailed away as Mercy was already marching down the hallway to Mr Burnhard's room. Mercy knew why animal control refused to come. Mr Henry Burnhard was a 90-year-old Bear Shifter, a resident of the Veteran's Hospital, who was losing his ability to control his shifting, something that happened to many older shifters. He was fairly harmless, except, of course, to humans, because he was able to turn into a 9-foot grizzly.

Mercy entered the room and immediately saw the grizzly, down on all fours, trying to snuffle extra meals from the meal cart. The extra meals were kept down below behind the cabinet doors, and as a bear, the elderly Shifter had forgotten how to open the cabinet, so he was banging the cart up against the wall with his paw.

"Mr. Burnhard, shift back to human and get back into bed right now," said Mercy sternly. "If you want extra food, all you have to do is ask. Beverly would've been glad to give you seconds. There's no need for this."

The problem with elderly Shifters was that their animal form was more *animal*. Like young pubescent Shifters, they were almost unable to maintain human cognition while in their other shape. Mr. Burnhard reared up on his hind feet to his full 9-foot height and roared at her. The display from his huge jars was properly intimidating. Or it would've been to a human woman.

Mercy, however, was a special form of shape shifter herself. She focused her will and switched her form.

Mercy transformed from a 5'3" woman into a towering Amazon almost 7 feet tall. Her weight was the same; but now, her extra fat was now all concentrated in her huge breasts which thrust out over her toned belly and broad hips. Her thighs were lean and muscular. And, as long as she had the bod to go with it, she figured she ought to dress the part; she wore a chain-mail bikini lined with fur and jewels. She wore gauntlets and grieves to match, and a helmet that was fitted to allow for her cranial wings. All Valkyries had these special wings, which extended on either side of the head instead of earlobes, called auricle feathers. Her hair no longer looked like a short brown bob, but a long flowing waterfall of platinum and gold. Honestly, the golden waterfall was not actually hair at all, but more feathers, but those feathers were so soft and long they looked like hair. She had a second pair of wings on her back as well, but these were enhanced by huge steel blade extensions. The combined diameter of her back wings and blades was 15 feet across. She also held a 11-foot spear tipped with metal forged in Valhalla.

Yeah. Her other form was a mother-ducking Valkyrie.

The bear immediately cringed, whined, and curled back up into the shape of an old man in a hospital gown.

"I'm sorry, Mercy," he muttered. "I don't know what got into me. I was just hungry..."

Turning into a Valkyrie always made Mercy hungry too, so she completely sympathized. She stayed in her Valkyrie form until he climbed back into bed. Then she also shrank back into her plump, brown-bobbed, hazel-eyed, human self, wearing pink and teal scrubs with a teddy bear pattern. She tucked Mr. Burnhard back into bed, salvaged what she could from the food cart, and set him up with a second lunch.

It was then that Mercy heard a soft gasp behind her. She world around. Beverly, the human who knew nothing about magic, was standing in the doorway.

"How long have you been there, Bev?" asked Mercy.

"The whole time," Beverly said. "I saw you confront the bear. And then it stood up on its legs and roared at you. And you just told it to behave itself and..." She looked around confused. Even though Bev had seen the bear become Mr. Burnhard right in front of her, her human mind would not accept what she had seen. She exhaled in relief as her mind came up with an explanation. "The bear ran off and Mr. Burnhard came out from behind the bed where he was hiding. Mercy, you're so brave!"

Mercy smiled. "I'm sure the bear was more afraid of me than I was of the bear."

~

June 17, Friday

Miles Malone had a mystery to solve. Who had killed... um, *tried* to kill... him?

Fortunately, if strangely, Miles had survived a fire blast to his chest, but someone had reported there was a corpse in the dumpster to the police.

Miles reviewed the facts of the case. Last month, on June 8, two people, an unrelated man and woman, Owen McGee and Eleni Bendox, had approached him to find out who had handcuffed them together and locked them in a car with no brakes that was pushed into a lake. A terrible incident, it was amazing the pair had survived. Miles had researched the case diligently, making it a priority above all his other work.

He found out who was behind it rather quickly. It was good luck for law enforcement when criminals were dumb. Miles was pleased with himself, although he wasn't certain his clients would be happy when they found out the truth.

However, when he'd tried to contact either Owen McGee or Eleni Bendox, the phone numbers proved to out of service. They had both given him burner phones.

Eleni contacted him on June 16; this time, she warned him not to trust Owen. Eleni said her life was in danger. She asked to meet Miles. Miles promised to give her the information about who had tried to kill her.

Eleni arrived to take the package, but Owen arrived a few minutes later, running toward her, yelling at her not to talk to Miles.

And that's when the bird-man appeared in the sky and attacked Miles.

Okay, so obviously, Miles had not been killed by a bird-man, a winged man, or a dark angel. Nonetheless, he hadn't punched *himself* in the chest and crawled into a dumpster for the fun of it. Someone had taken a pot shot at him.

Owen McGee?

At first, that seemed the obvious choice. Owen wanted to keep Eleni from finding out what Miles knew, so Owen shot him. The third man, the "dark angel," was nothing but a hallucination.

But it didn't fit. Owen hadn't been armed. And... it wasn't consistent with what Miles remembered.

If only what Miles remembered wasn't impossible.

Miles phoned the office of Eleni Bendox. She was a US District Attorney. If either Owen, or the mystery third man, or the one who had attacked Owen and Eleni in the first place, might have tried to harm her again. Miles wanted to be sure she was safe.

"I'm sorry, she hasn't been in the office since last Monday," her assistant reported.

"Thank you," said Miles, more disturbed than before.

He decided to send an email as well, so he checked her website to find it. There, featured rather prominently on the site, was a photo of Eleni Bendox, in a suit, standing next to a striking dark-haired man in judge's black robes. The photo was from an online news article with the headline: *Federal Prose-*

cutor Joins Special Arcana Glen District. Pictured, from left to right, US District Attorney Eleni Bendox with Judge Raziel Ranaci. (Courtesy photo). The photo was from more than a decade ago, but Eleni Bendox looked exactly the same, like a gorgeous woman in her late twenties or early thirties.

The other man hadn't changed either—and Miles Malone recognized him.

Judge Raziel Ranaci was the man who had tried to kill him.

~

June 23, Thursday

Miles didn't pursue the case of his own attempted murder as diligently as he did other cases. He confirmed for two seperate clients that each of their wives were cheating, it turned out, with each other's husbands. He was paid by both clients and didn't disclose the irony to either, although he lost all sympathy for the cuckholds who were themselves unfaithful.

He told himself that it was more important to work on those cases than his own issue because he needed the money, but he still barely had enough to pay the mortgage.

On Thursday, through no effort of his own, he made a breakthrough in his private case. Eleni Bendox finally returned his call.

"Ms Bendox, I'm relieved to discover you are still with us," said Miles frankly. "I was beginning to think something had happened to you."

"Mr Malone!" she said, sounding amused. "Here I thought I was the one who was worried about you! I can't tell you how shocked and pleased I was to discover you are alive. I feared the worst."

After he realized who had called, Miles searched his computer to stare once again at the picture of Eleni Bendox and Judge Raziel Ranaci.

"On the day I tried to meet with you, I was attacked," Miles said mildly, as if reporting that it had rained, and he'd had pastrami for lunch. "Do you have any idea who did it?"

A pause.

Would she lie to him?

Miles really hoped she wasn't in on it. He hated it when beautiful women turned out to be no good. It was such a waste.

"What do remember?" she asked cautiously.

"Nothing after meeting you but before waking up in a dumpster," he lied. It was partially true. He remembered nothing sane.

"A former co-worker of mine attacked you," she said. Her voice was tight. "Raziel Ranaci. He used to be a judge, but he... fell from grace. Don't worry about him attacking you again, however. He was apprehended and is being punished."

"Oh," said Miles, taken aback. 'Apprehended' and 'punished,' was an odd way to say, 'arrested and convicted,' but what else could she mean? "Thank you."

"Thank *you*. Thanks to the information you gave me, I was also able to deal with the other matter."

Again, oddly vague.

"What about Owen McGee?" asked Miles. "Is he a threat to you?"

"No... no, that was a misunderstanding," she said quickly. "Also resolved."

Resolved how? She wouldn't say, even when Miles pressed her for more details.

Miles thanked her again, she thanked him again, and they hung up.

The mystery of Miles Malone's near-murder had been solved and his murderer was apparently 'being punished.' Miles should have felt happy that the whole affair had been wrapped up.

Instead, he felt uneasy, as if he was missing the most important thing.

Three

June 27, Monday

MILES MALONE HAD an appointment at 10 o'clock with a potential client. Her name was Gini Brown. Eva White had talked to her on the phone to make the appointment. Eva conveyed the impression that Ms Brown was a widow. Miles was anticipating an older, hopefully wealthy woman, who might pay good money to see if her young boy toy was cheating on her.

He was somewhat disappointed that the woman who entered was young and pretty and not wearing expensive clothes.

"I really need your help, detective," she said in a soft, sad voice. "I think someone murdered my boyfriend. I can't afford to pay you very much. But the police won't take me seriously at all." She looked angry. "You know how small-town police are. Completely useless."

Apparently, this was going to be one of those cases that Miles took out of a sense of obligation to help a damsel in distress, and not a case in which he would be able to milk a rich woman for money to pay his secretary and his mortgage. But what could he do? The girl looked at him with big doe eyes and he found himself saying, "Tell me exactly why you think he was murdered but the police don't."

"He died during surgery. Gawain just needed surgery on an injury he got while serving overseas. It wasn't a big deal, and he was young and strong. Yet he died on the operating table from some medical issue totally unrelated to what he was in surgery for. Doesn't that seem suspicious to you, Detective Malone?"

"Maybe what you need is a medical malfeasance lawyer. You could sue the doctor..."

"I don't think his doctor is responsible!" cried Gini Brown. "Gawain's doctor is wonderful; he's saved so many lives. Gawain had nothing but good things to say about Dr Winters. In fact, it was Winters who warned him that he should probably move to a better facility because there have been a lot of mysterious deaths where he was."

"Go on," said Miles.

"Well, that's really all I know. My boyfriend was kind of psychic, you know?"

Miles studiously kept his face from showing his skepticism. He believed in the existence of real psychics like he believed in the existence of honest politicians.

"And my boyfriend said that he thought one of the nurses was involved. He called her an angel of death."

"Were those his exact words? *An* angel of death? Or did he say, '*the* angel of death'?"

"Oh, I'm not sure... Is there more than one?"

"I was going to ask you that, Ms Brown. I don't have a psychic boyfriend."

"I don't know. But I need to find out if someone killed him. If you could just find enough evidence that the police would take the case seriously. I will pay you. Do you take credit?"

"Yes, I can take credit cards."

"I wasn't really thinking of a card, so much is I would, uh, promise to pay you in the future. I work as a waitress and during the summer I get a lot of tips. I'm going to give all of them to you."

Miles struggled with his conscience. Probably there was nothing to this so-called murder beyond the reluctance of a troubled girl to accept the death of her young soldier boyfriend. She clearly didn't have the money to pay him, so he would probably just end up doing it *pro bono*.

That would waste time he could spend on other cases. Not that he had any other cases at the moment. He convinced himself a little *pro bono* work might drum up other business. Satisfied he had a reason to accept the case, he nodded.

"Tell me more about the hospital where your boyfriend was staying," said Miles. "I didn't even know there was a hospital here in Arcana Glen."

"You'd be surprised what's here in Arcana Glen," said Gini a bit coyly. "All sorts of stuff turns up where you don't expect it."

June 27, Monday

Miles pulled into the guest parking at the Veterans' Hospital. It was tucked away on a curvy mountain road surrounded by trees. It was a peaceful location, much nicer than hospitals he remembered from trips to the emergency room in the city. It still didn't make sense to him that there would be an entire veterans' hospital in a two-bit town hidden in the mountains. A sanatorium for rich people, maybe, but this pleasant L-shaped two-story building was nicer than he expected.

He reviewed the facts of the case he was able to squeeze out of Gini Brown. The victim, if indeed he was a victim, was Gawain Herle, age twenty-four, one hundred seventy pounds, brown eyes, brown hair.

Gawain had been injured in the Middle East, breaking his left leg. The leg was initially dressed in Germany, but for some strange reason, Gawain Herle was flown to Arcana Glen. Not Walters Reed in Denver. Arcana Glen—a pin-prick town in the Rocky Mountains.

There, Gawain was assigned to the care of a physician named Dr Richard Sharpe. His nurse was Beverly Howard.

Gawain Herle, in surgery to have a pin inserted in his leg, died of coronary failure.

Gawain Herle had no living relatives. In fact, his relationship with Gini had only started three weeks before he went overseas.

Miles headed for the entrance of the hospital. Inside, it smelled like antiseptic, as one would expect from a hospital, and everything was neat and clean. There were cute murals on the wall, signed by the class from the local public high school. The murals portrayed animals in uniform, as if they were soldiers: Airforce eagles, Army wolves, Navy Seals who were actual seals and so on. Cute.

He checked the front directory and found the names of the doctors and nurses he wanted to visit. There were a dozen nurses, but only three doctors listed: Dr Warren Winters, Dr Richard Sharpe, and Dr August Cornel.

Miles was on his way to the second floor when he passed a woman that looked familiar. He stopped in his tracks and frankly stared at her.

She wasn't classically beautiful, but she was adorable. She wore the unflattering scrubs of a registered nurse: teal slacks and a white blouse with pink and teal teddy bears. She had soft, squeezable curves. A bob of brown hair fell just below her ears. Her eyes were hazel and sparkled with laughter as she talked with another older nurse. He had a good memory, even an eidetic memory for faces, but although he was certain he had seen her before, he couldn't place her in any context. It was going to bug him for the rest of the day if he did not find out who she was.

He started to walk towards her, but then she turned away and went into another part of the hospital. She had never looked in his direction. He figured she was busy and now would not be a good time to go chasing after her. He kind of hoped she was nurse Beverly Howard, the only nurse on his list.

He found Dr Winters first, the doctor that Gini Brown had raved about. He was a tall thin man, with sharp eyes and a sharp nose. His hair was wispy and silver, although he looked too young to be turning gray. Miles found it unusually difficult to determine the man's age. Winters had an air of authority that suggested many decades of expertise and surgical experience: but he had no wrinkles around his eyes or his forehead, not even smile lines. If not for his imperious manner, Miles would have thought he was an intern in his twenties. But if Miles had only heard the barking commands that Winters gave to his staff, Miles would've assumed that Dr Winters was in his 60s, verging on the age when he would be best described as a grumpy old man. Finally, Miles figured Winters must be somewhere in his 50s: satisfied with his own performance and impatient with the mistakes of others. Miles often tried to soften up subjects with a few jokes, but he sensed this would backfire with Winters. So Miles kept his demeanor businesslike.

"Excuse me, Dr Winters? I'd like to talk to you about a recent case of yours. A young man. I understand he was here for routine surgery, but something happened with his heart. The patient's name was Gawain Herle."

Dr Winters looked annoyed. "Who are you?"

"I was wondering if you think the primary physician was to blame," Miles said hoping to distract him and also throw him some raw meat to see if he would bite.

"Dr. Sharpe is a good physician and a good man," said Dr Winters testily. "But he is a general practitioner. When he realized that the patient had an undiagnosed heart problem, he called me in. I'm a specialist and I did what I could but, unfortunately, in this case, it was too late. I'm afraid I can't divulge any medical details beyond that. Now, I suggest you leave, sir."

~

Miles did not want Dr Winters to call security, so he extracted himself from that conversation and pursued Dr. Sharpe, the general practitioner. Dr. Sharpe was more friendly.

With Sharpe, Miles knew he could create camaraderie with a few jokes.

"Is it true that they eyes are the last part of the body to die?" Miles asked innocently. "Because I've heard the pupils dilate."

Dr Sharpe laughed, "That's a good one, I'll have to remember that to share with my patients."

He invited Miles into his office and pontificated for a long while on the nature of medicine in general. He took much longer to give less information than Dr Winters had given in a few sentences.

The mutual admiration society continued here. Dr Sharpe had nothing but good things to say about Dr Winters.

"Of course," admitted Sharpe, "Winters is good, but he's no Cornel."

"Cornel?" asked Miles. "Do you mean Dr August Cornel, your third colleague here?"

Dr Sharpe nodded. He leaned forward and said confidentially, "Don't tell Winters I told you that though. He's already jealous enough of Cornel."

"Was Dr. Cornel involved in this case?"

"No. If he had been, maybe the boy would've been saved. He's a specialist, like Winters, but he's the best. I'm not saying Winters is bad, but he's no Cornel. Cornel is a miracle worker," Dr. Sharpe raved. "He's saved many patients we thought could not be saved. If only he had been there... But it was his day off. Winters was on call."

Miles asked some more questions because Dr Sharpe was talkative, but he continued to be less than helpful when it came to the details. Finally, Dr Sharpe said, "I have to tell you something. The truth is, this is a hospital, and people die. It's sad. It's something we don't like to think about. As doctors, it hurts us to lose anyone. But we are dealing with people who come to us with severe problems, some diagnosed, and some not. I don't know if you knew this, but our hospital is kind of considered a last stop for some patients, for a special class of veterans."

"A special class of veterans?" Miles perked up at this. "And what class would that be?"

"Veterans who have been refused medical treatment anywhere else. For whatever reason."

"What reason would there be... as an example?"

Dr Sharpe waved his hands vaguely. "For whatever reason. They come to us, and we are able to offer them treatment they can't get anywhere else. But sometimes they come to us too late, and sometimes they don't tell us everything that is wrong. We do lose some good men. That's how it goes. Death is part of life, Miles. May I call you Miles? Death is the other half of life, and Death always wins in the end."

"Not always." Miles thought of how he had awakened in a dumpster not long ago, with a big hole in his chest where his heart and lungs ought to have been.

Dr Sharpe gave him a weird look.

"Not right away," amended Miles. "The important thing is not to go into the darkness without a fight."

"Of course," said Dr Sharpe, with an amused smile. "Fight death as long as you can, but don't lay bets on the final round."

Four

June 28, 2022

MERCY SMILED at the handsome young soldier in the bed. His name was Miguel Ramos and he was a Coyote shifter. As a Valkyrie, a specialist branch of the reaper species, Mercy had a form of magic known as Deathsense. Some reapers preferred to call it *the Life Meter*, to focus on the positive aspect. To Mercy, it didn't matter because life and death were two halves of one whole. Death was not a termination, but a destination, a gateway to the next location or reincarnation where a spirit would exist. Since she had seen the place where she escorted her clients, she never felt any guilt about opening the Door for those she knew were Called. Not all reapers were so lucky. Reapers specialized in reaping different kinds of souls. As a Valkyrie, she only took souls who had died honorably in battle, and she opened a Door for them to Valhalla. Valhalla wasn't everyone's idea of paradise, but for those who enjoyed a little more roughhousing than strumming harps beside peaceful waterfalls, it was pretty dang awesome.

Mercy's Deathsense was a balanced mix of Dark and Light magic, or what, in some traditions, one would call Yin and Yang. She didn't know how it worked for other reapers, but for her, and for all the Valkyries in her family, she saw the image of an hourglass superimposed over every living being with a soul. The hourglass showed how much lifeforce an individual possessed. It wasn't a countdown to their days remaining to spend on earth. It was a measure of their current vitality.

In that way, maybe "Life Meter" was a better metaphor than an Hourglass, but a reaper didn't consciously choose how their Deathsense manifested. The important thing was that her vision of the Hourglass was not a *prediction* of the future, only a *measure* of how much health and life remaining a person had at the current moment. As a Valkyrie, Mercy did not have a gift of prophecy, only of diagnosis.

When she had first seen Miguel Ramos, he had not only suffered an injury to his arm, but he had felt sad and isolated after the death of several Coyotes who were both pack mates and members of his squad. The sand in the upper cup of his Hourglass had been perilously low.

After some time in the hospital, during which she tried to cheer him up and help put him in touch with others in the Shifter community here in Arcana Glen, including some vets, his mood improved. His Hourglass changed to reflect that. The sand in the upper half soon showed a degree of fullness that suited a man of his age and physical health. Now that his arm was healing, he had even more sand in the top of his Hourglass then below, which meant a long life awaited him—as long as nothing else changed.

She was pleased to see that both her mystical insight, and his medical chart at the end of the bed, converged on this happy diagnosis. She examined the cast on his arm, which had been newly set. "Are you about ready for that thing to come off?"

"Ready?" Ramos made a funny face. "I was ready three weeks ago! Why do I have to wear the cast so long when I heal faster than a normal human?"

"Standard procedure. And for your information, you already have been greatly accelerated from what most men in your position would have to expect. If you'd been human, we probably would've needed to amputate your arm and replace it with a prosthetic. Not that losing an arm would've been the end of the world. You should know some Shifters do have prosthetics. But in your case, that won't be necessary. You're healing like a real trooper."

He answered her smile with a shy smile of his own. "Will you finally agree to date to me after I leave here, Mercy?"

"You flirt. I bet you have three girlfriends already."

"Sure, but none of them are as cute as you."

They shared a laugh.

"Mercy, I've been trying this whole time to figure out what kind of Shifter you are. I hoped you were a Coyote so I could bring you home to mama. But now I think I figured it out."

"Oh?" She smiled and waited. Usually, other Shifters had a hard time figuring her out. Sometimes even other reapers did not recognize her kind.

"You're an angel. And I know where your parents got your name."

"My name was a suggestion from my fairy godmother," said Mercy. She wasn't joking; she had a fairy godmother, and thank goodness, because otherwise her parents' ideas about what to name her would have prevailed. "My parents wanted to name me Skalda!"

After she checked on Miguel Ramos, Mercy checked on another patient she was concerned about. Unfortunately, Tony Ban was in much worse shape. She didn't know as much about his military background, even though, ironically, he had not been stationed overseas but had served right here at the base in Arcana Glen. The base was very secretive, and it was unusual to have soldiers from there at this veterans' hospital. He had been sent here because the ambulance had picked the closest hospital with an emergency room.

He had been in some kind of fire fight. That was strange because, again, as far as she knew, he had not been in active combat. But when he muttered about dragons in his sleep, she wondered if he had gotten into a local fight with the Dragon population that she knew lived in town. It was strange, because she hadn't heard anything about that in the news, not even the news that catered to the arcanes.

With both physical injuries to his bones and burns over most of his body, combined with the fact that he was mundane, not a Shifter or other form of supernatural, the chances he would survive were low. It was all the more heartbreaking because he was conscious some of the time. He was very bitter and angry about what had happened to him, although he would not say what it was. If he really had been attacked by a Dragon Shifter, he might have remembered the incident. Being burnt by a dragon was not the same as seeing a man change into a bear. It was traumatic enough that it would convert even the most resistant mundane into a believer in magic. But belief didn't give mundanes the power to heal from the dire impact of such magic.

Tony Ban was asleep when she visited him. Mercy knew better than to wake him up. She quietly checked his chart. The Hourglass, which she perceived like a holograph hovering, superimposed, over his sleeping form, showed very little sand remaining in the top cup. The grains of sand were moving slowly.

That meant he was struggling against the darkness he could feel creeping toward him. Good—at least his was fighting for life. Although she herself accepted death and knew that what awaited her soldiers on the other side was a better world, that didn't mean she wanted them to rush toward it. It was one of those ironies. Those who hurried towards death, hoping for something better, seldom found something pleasant on the other side, whereas those who held on, those who loved life and fought for it, were the very ones who are most likely to love what they found on the other side as well.

She made the rest of her rounds more quickly. Most of the men in the hospital were in between the extremes of Ramos and Ban. She saw their Hourglasses in varying degrees of partly full, partly emptied out, but knew that could change depending on how their operations went or how their illnesses progressed.

She was finishing up when she noticed a man sitting in Dr. Sharpe's office. The man had his back to the door and Dr. Sharpe was talking his ear off as he was wont to do with anyone who would indulge him. It didn't matter that the man could not see her, she could see the Hourglass over his body just as well as if he had been facing her. But there was something extraordinarily strange about his Hourglass.

Most Hourglasses that she saw looked like the classic figure 8, with a broad cup on top, a matching inverted cup on the bottom, a wasp waist, and a solid top and stand. The Hourglass used by the Wicked Witch of the West in the 1939 Wizard of Oz movie was close to what Mercy saw (possibly even her subconscious inspiration), although those in her vision were a ghostly white, not colorful. The sand was luminous and silvery, as if each grain was a sparkling diamond, a beautiful particle of life, a gemstone to be cherished like a treasure.

The man talking to Dr. Sharpe had an Hourglass, like every living being. But his was not shaped like a figure 8. It was shaped like an infinity sign. It was lying on its side, with the two portions parallel to each other and the narrow spot in the middle connecting them like a bridge. The sand flowed, in constant motion, yet never ran out from either side. The diamond crystal dust surged back and forth like a gentle sea across the sign of infinity.

Mercy had never seen anything like it. She must have gasped, for suddenly the man turned around and saw her.

The heat that warmed her cheeks had nothing to do with her embarrassment at being caught staring at his weird Hourglass. Instead, she could hardly even see it any longer because she was now focused entirely on his physical form. He was rugged and sexy and had a little quirk to his smile that made her heart stop. He wore a casual shirt and Dockers. His attire did not hide that he was completely ripped. In fact, she could make the faint outline under his shirt of a muscular chest with chiseled pecks and abs.

"I am... I'm sorry... You're busy and... I'll just..."

Mercy hurried away from the office.

"Wait!" the man cried.

She almost broke into a run. She did not know if he realized she had seen there was something strange about his Hourglass, or if he noticed her drooling over his physical charms like a schoolgirl. Either way she was too embarrassed to find out what he wanted.

"Wait!" he cried again. "Are you by any chance Beverly Howard?"

Relief and disappointment went to war inside her chest, causing her heart to beat wildly. He didn't want to talk to her at all!

"No!" She shouted it over her shoulder. "But I'll get her for you!"

Grasping that excuse with both hands like a football final moments of the quarter, Mercy took off running down the corridor.

Five

June 29, Wednesday

BACK IN HIS office the next day, Miles kept thinking about the adorable brunette nurse who had run from him when he tried to call her. Did she recognize him as well? He still couldn't place where he had seen her before.

When he had first turned around, she had been staring at him with an expression of shock. It wasn't exactly recognition, though. More like she had seen Miles standing on his head and wondered what the hell he was doing upside down.

Thinking about her wasn't going to close the case. What he was *supposed* to be doing today was going through records. This was the part of the job that was tedious but necessary. It required careful attention to detail, because if he missed something the first time he went through the paperwork he wouldn't have time to go through everything again. So, he had learned to be patient and read carefully. If somethings struck him as odd, he made a note of it, even if he could not tell yet whether it would be useful in the future.

He researched all the paperwork he could access on Gawain Herle,

Gini Brown's deceased boyfriend. Miles went through autopsy reports, birth and death records, service records, and background information. He found a few interesting coincidences. For instance, both at Gawain's high school, and in his military unit, he had acquired the nickname "the Centaur." Strange. Maybe he had told his buddies in the military what his high school nickname had been? There was no way anybody would come up with that twice. Unless the guy was really enthusiastic about a Sagittarius birthday. But Gawain wasn't a Sagittarius.

Other than that, Miles couldn't find much. Gawain had been an average student, a good kid, with no criminal record, a clean but unexciting record of military service. Gawain's injury was the most interesting thing about him. He had stepped on an IED but somehow survived with nothing more than a broken leg. One of the reports said "broken hind leg," which Miles made a note of because it was strange to use the term "hind leg" for a human. Was it a joke or an error? Most likely, it wasn't important.

Miles scratched his head. Nothing extraordinary was coming to him about this case. Guy had a leg injury, went into surgery, and died of a heart problem. The heart problem had been congenital but not diagnosed until it caused problems on the operating table. Tragic, but not inexplicable.

When Miles couldn't stand staring at the paperwork anymore, he decided to go out for a run. That was what had really sold him on staying in Arcana Glen. He might've been annoyed by the small-town stand-offishness, but he freaking loved being so close to the forest. Near his townhouse office was a nature trail. It wasn't so far from town that he couldn't drive back to Main Street if he got an important call, yet once he was out amongst the trees he felt as though he were in the middle of a wilderness.

Well not quite wilderness. The other thing he liked about the nature trail was that it was marked at regular intervals by outdoor gym stations. There were bars for pull ups, push-ups, benches for sit ups and so on. If you wanted to lift weights you had to bring your own.

Perhaps because there were so many performers who lived in Arcana Glen, members of the Enchanted Circus who performed at the local casino, there were also more unusual pieces of equipment along the nature trail. There were two trees with a high bar positioned such that a man could hang from them and flip around. Miles was no acrobat, but he had seriously studied yoga. Not for the spiritual side, because he wasn't that kind of guy, but because he completely believed in the health benefits.

There was something about physical activity that helped a man focus his mind. When he was flexing his body and stretching his muscles, experiencing the flow of energy through his limbs in a new way, new ideas came to him about old problems. He liked to literally hang upside down from the high bar, first with one leg, then the other, sometimes with both, and stare at things from the viewpoint of a bat. Just flipping himself around physically sometimes had amazing effects on his ability to look at things from a new perspective.

~

June 29, Wednesday

Usually, Miles did the nature trail exercise circuit alone, but if he happened to meet up with another guy that he met out there some-times, sometimes they would do the circuit together. Today he met John Helwall just as they were both at the head of the trail. John was a construction worker, with the body of a pro-wrestler. Nearly seven feet tall, he was huge and bulky and looked as though he could crush anvils in one hand just for fun. Nature hadn't done him any favors with that classic mafia-thug henchman mug. Yet it was the kind of face which women sometimes found appealing for a reason Miles could not understand, with a very square jaw, cleft chin, and assortment of thin, disreputable looking scars across his broken nose and ice-cold blue eyes.

Despite his appearance as a hitman out of Central Casting, John was always friendly with Miles.

"Hey," said John. "I brought some weights this time. Do you want to spot me?"

"Sure," said Miles. "Where are the weights?"

"Oh…" John looked around vaguely. "I already put them out there earlier. We'll get them when we get to the weight station."

Sure enough, when they got to the weight station, John procured a series of iron barbells from behind one of the trees. Miles wanted to ask him if he was crazy to leave such an expensive weight set out here in the wilderness with no security, but then he considered who would dare steal something from the giant and decided, probably John was fine.

Miles spotted John as he lifted an insane number of pounds. Then John helped Miles struggle with about 1/10 the weight of that. Miles was melting by the time he was done. John didn't have a bead of perspiration on him. He still looked as cool as ice despite the fact that the July morning was starting to heat up.

However, when they reached the high bar, Miles had his revenge. He clambered up like a monkey and hung from one leg. John shook his head.

"Just watching you do that makes me sick to my stomach," he admitted.

"Yoga," said Miles.

"Isn't that just something women do in tight leotards?" asked John.

"Just an added benefit," said Miles and winked. They smirked at each other.

"I could never get my body to do that," John said. "I think if I bent my body like that, it would just break."

"I used to think I was no good at yoga either," Miles admitted. "I felt like a real poser."

John groaned.

"But then I found a great yoga teacher," Miles continued merrily, "Yeah, she really bent over backwards for me!"

"Are you married?" asked John. "I remember you saying something about your wife."

"Ex-wife. I'm not looking for number two. How about you?"

"In my culture, arranged marriages are expected. My clan will probably find a wench for me, and I won't have much choice about it. But they also won't care if I have fun on the side, so it's okay." He shrugged.

"Your culture?" Miles asked. This was one of those weird things he kept encountering in Arcana Glen. People acted like they were from another planet or something, but when you pressed them on it, they backed off and pretended they hadn't said anything strange. "Aren't you from Iceland? Do they still have arranged marriages in Iceland?"

And just as Miles expected, John changed the subject, and they moved onto the next station.

~

June 29, Wednesday

When Mercy got home, she found a ghost waiting for her. Not just any ghost either, a ghost centaur. Worse, she recognized him. She had never seen him in his centaur form, although she had heard that was what he was from the other arcanes. But his human half was identical to his human self as a man, so it wasn't hard to see this was the ghost of Gawain Herle.

"Mercy," he said, "I came to warn you."

"Warn me? What's wrong, Gawain?"

"It's Ramos. He's in trouble. You need to get to the hospital right away before the Bad One gets to him."

Mercy had been about to put down her satchel and take off her nursing orthopedic sneakers. She changed her mind and headed back out the door.

As she rode her bike, he started galloping alongside her, about a foot above the ground. Although she was not moving anywhere near the speed of a gallop, he stayed abreast of her.

"Who is the Bad One?" she asked.

"The one who took me before my time. You know it wasn't my time, Mercy. You could tell. That's why I'm a ghost. I wasn't supposed to go through the Door yet, and now I don't have a Door."

Pain contorted his face. "What am I supposed to do now? How am I supposed to get where I need to go if I no longer have a passageway? Can you help me?"

"I will try," she promised. But she had a sinking feeling about it. She was supposed to take her clients at the moment of their death. She wasn't really a necromancer, prepared to deal with ghosts or other unsettled spirits.

~

June 29, Wednesday

For the first time, Mercy wished she had something faster than a bicycle. She peddled as hard as she could, but she sensed that danger was approaching faster than she was progressing. She hurried into the hospital and almost ran to Miguel Ramos's room, even though the night staff stared at her in astonishment.

She popped open the door and took in the neatly made empty bed.

She was too late.

Just in case he had only been moved, she looked for the on-duty nurse and confirmed that he had passed during the night. Cardiac arrest. By the time the on-call doctor, Dr Cornel, had arrived, there was nothing anyone could do for him.

"And you know that if Cornel couldn't do anything, no one could," added the nurse. She shook her head. "Poor boy. He was so young, and he looked like he was healing so well. Who knew he had a heart problem?"

"Doesn't it seem like an awful lot of our patients have undiagnosed heart problems that prove fatal?" Mercy asked slowly.

"It's just a coincidence, Mercy," shrugged the nurse.

Mercy huffed in frustration. The woman was mundane, and although nice, not at all sensitive to magic or unusual phenomenon. Apparently, she wasn't very aware of unusual patterns of any kind. She was going to shrug this off in the same way that she would stare directly at a shape shifter turning into an animal and convince herself she had seen something else.

Mercy studied the chart available on Ramos, but she couldn't find anything that added up to his sudden heart failure. The whole thing was so bewildering.

Trying to cheer her up, the nurse said brightly, "But we did have one

good save today. Dr Cornel was able to operate on the burn patient...
You know..."

"Tony Ban?"

"Yeah! Him. He was completely cured and released from the hospital today."

"But he had severe burns all over his body!"

"I know it's like a miracle. Isn't Dr Cornel amazing?"

Six

June 30, Thursday

MERCY LOOKED at the records and found that Dr Cornel had been the attending physician for Tony Ban. Dr Sharpe had been the attending physician for Ramos. But what really caught her attention was that Ramos had died at the same moment that Ban had his miraculous recovery.

Could magic be involved? Could someone have attempted to swap the life force of one man for the other?

Although dark magic did not have to be used for evil purposes, unfortunately there were wizards who found it easy to use the shadowy, chthonic powers involved in dark magic for their own selfish gain. But both Dr Cornel and Dr Sharpe were human. As far as she knew, neither had any magic. Dr Sharpe was completely mundane, whereas Cornel, she suspected, was a sensitive.

On her break, Mercy went outside the hospital. Usually, smokers came out the back door for a cigarette break because they weren't supposed to smoke inside. However, there weren't many staff who smoked these days, so she had the back porch to herself. Softly she called out to the ghost Gawain Herle.

The centaur appeared to her, floating slightly above the earth instead of standing on it, almost translucent. Next to him was another ghost, Miguel Ramos.

"Both of you died recently," she said, "So I'm going to try to cross you over. I can't promise it will work."

Because she was nervous, she was tempted to over-explain. She wanted to tell them that she usually relied on an old reaper hack, using the momentum of the soul's first snap as it separated from the body, to propel the spirit into the door. To create a Door "cold" was a much more challenging task, usually only achieved by reapers after decades of practice. Mercy was pretty much the same age she looked as a human, in her mid-30s. Of course, she would live for much longer than an ordinary human; if she could see her own Hourglass, (she could not but her mother could), she would see many grains of sand in the upper cup falling very slowly to a small pile below.

However, her clients didn't want to hear all of this. She would save up her thoughts and share them at the upcoming reaper convention. For once it was going to be held nearby, right here in Arcana Glen, so she could afford to take the time and go.

Gawain and Miguel were still looking at her expectantly. She didn't want to break their ghostly hearts by failing them. She took a deep breath and summoned a Door.

To her delight, a Door appeared. It looked like an ordinary, if somewhat old and decrepit wooden door in a frame, standing alone in the middle of the field.

She squealed and clapped her hands. "I did it!"

The two ghosts exchanged a look.

"Are you sure that's the right Door?" asked Gawain, studying the battered wooden door skeptically.

"Yeah," said Miguel. "It looks more like a door to Chicago then to Valhalla."

"Hey!" protested Mercy. "A Door is a Door."

Sure, with chipped paint and worn-out wood, it did look as if it had seen better days. But that was completely irrelevant to what mattered.

"Can't you feel the energy?" she asked the ghosts. "It's bright, but it's exciting. This door leads to Valhalla. I can show you. I will lead you there. You won't be alone. I will be by your side as you travel through to the New World."

She held out both of her hands and one ghost took each hand. Then she assumed her Valkyrie shape. The door creaked open on its own, and through the rectangular frame, they could all see what lay beyond.

Valhalla was just one of many realms that were a part of the great luminous sphere of Dayhaven. The endless glowing skies of Dayhaven never knew the shadow of night. Huge islands floated in a glowing empyrean, drifting gently amid clouds, sliding by one another, and yet never colliding, so that the winged beings who lived there could visit friends in other paradises.

Most of the floating islands were peaceful and verdant, bursting with gardens, teaming with rivers and waterfalls, bedazzled with mansions and palaces. Valhalla was more rugged than most. The mountains were taller, and the caverns dripping below the subterranean part of the island into the sky were deeper. There was snow on the peaks, and dungeons in the depths, but this rough land was not a place of punishment; it was an adventure park for warriors who wanted to enjoy battles with mindless elemental monsters, merely to test their mettle. The Warriors on the island still wore their battle gear, or donned new armor in whatever historical style they fancied. Valhalla was like a living video game for them, where their avatars were immortal bodies, and the enemies were the negative aspects of their own souls, magically given physical form and matched to the level of the spiritual warrior fighting them, so that gradually, through physical combat, they could conquer their own demons.

Those who are called to Valhalla were not perfect men and women, they were good men and women who wanted to be better. In Valhalla they were given a chance to do so in the way they had learned best in life, through combat. But no innocents perished, and no other good souls died in the battle. The only evil they had left to fight there were the remaining imperfections of their own spirits. When at last the Warriors were ready, and no longer needed the sport that a place like Valhalla offered, their spirits would relinquish their hold on that life and move on to a different portion of Paradise, or perhaps, if they were ready, to the Last Home.

Mercy flew with the ghosts through the door. As they emerged into Dayhaven, their translucent material forms were clothed in new, solid bodies, strongly muscular and wearing the uniforms they knew best. It was always a curiosity to Mercy whether the souls she escorted would come through at the same age they had been in the Mundane Sphere, or accept rebirth as an infant in the new Sphere. Either was possible, and it was not something that she controlled.

She did notice a pattern. Those who died young and had not experienced a full lifetime on earth were more likely to want to continue their current life to its proper end. Those who died after a long human life were eager to start anew. But each case was unique and depended so much upon the individual.

Much of magic was like that.

She landed them in Odin's fortress, a large Viking-style castle near the upper echelons of Valhalla. Odin had once been a man on earth, a human chieftain; then he had become a *Sarmat*, a Guardian, revered as divine by his former people. He had served as the Hanged Man, Guardian of the Twelfth Path. His sister, Hel, had also been a Guardian, the Guardian of Death, the Thirteenth Path. Hel had been one of the first Reapers, who discovered and passed on many of their arts.

~

June 30, Thursday

After Mercy delivered the ghosts, who were no longer ghosts but solid men with wings of steel, she planned to just start back to the Mundane Sphere as quickly as possible. But someone called out her name.

"Mercy!"

Mercy turned around. There was no point trying to hide now. A terrifying Valkyrie, seven feet tall, with flaming red feather hair, huge ear feathers and bronze metal wings bore down on Mercy like an unstoppable juggernaut. The hulking amazon wrapped her arms around Mercy and squeezed.

If Mercy hadn't been in her Valkyrie form as well, the hug would have broken her ribs.

"Hello, Mama," Mercy said.

"Maurice! Maurice, look who came to visit us," her mother, Guldra, shouted at Maurice, her father. "You never come to dinner," Mama complained, examining her with growing concern. "Look at you! You're so skinny. You're going to die of starvation if you don't eat something. Being a Valkyrie..."

"...Takes a lot of calories, yes, I know, Mama, look, I'm sorry, I can't stay. I actually just stepped through the door at work..."

"Well, of course you did, your work is to fly through the Door."

"No, I mean my other work. At the hospital, as a nurse."

"Oh *that*," said her mother rolling her eyes. "Ach, it's not as if that human work really matters, does it? Nothing you can't put aside to have dinner with your mother and father who haven't seen you in forever."

"I had dinner with you last Friday. And I'll be here tomorrow night."

"You know time flows differently here. It's been at least three centuries for me."

"Mama, that's not true..."

Her father finally ambled over. He adjusted his spectacles on his nose. In some ways, her parent's marriage was a classic Valkyrie love story. Her mother had fallen in love with one of the Warriors she ripped from the field of battle. But in the case of her parents, her father had worked in Naval Intelligence, and he wasn't exactly the stereotype of the beefy Viking. Of course, he could have changed his body here if he had wanted to, but he was stubborn and proud. He held onto his short stature, his nearsightedness, the spectacles he wore to correct it, and his bald head and beak of a nose.

"Felt like three hundred years to me too, believe me," Maurice Wise said.

"There's a new Warrior who arrived," Mama continued, ignoring him even though she had called him over. "Amanda brought him in... You remember Amanda, don't you honey? That tall girl, the daughter of Lumara? I keep telling you that you should ask what she does with her hair so you can try the same style. You might have more luck with men if you did something nice with your hair for once. Anyway, she brought in a Warrior I think you are going to love. I invited him to *Sebutu* dinner, and I would like you to meet him…"

"No!" Mercy rolled her eyes. "I told you. No more blind dates. And I'm not going to marry a Warrior who has already passed to Valhalla."

"But honey, it worked out so well for us."

"And I love that you guys found true love. I want that too. But right now, I have to get back to my job, okay?"

Before her mother could object or her father could crack a joke, she pecked both of them on the cheek, opened the door, and escaped back to the porch of the hospital.

June 30, Thursday

Out of habit, Mercy looked around when she arrived back on Earth to see if anyone had noticed her popping in and out of thin air. That's how it would've looked to an observer. Only the Warrior who was about to pass, and Mercy herself, could see the doors she formed. It wasn't like the kind of portal a Guardian could create, that anyone could use.

She didn't expect to see anyone, so when she turned around and almost bumped into Dr Winters, she emitted a little squeal of surprise.

"Dr Winters! I didn't see you there."

"Don't mind me," he said. "I just came out for a breath of fresh air. I see you did the same."

"Yes. Absolutely." She peered at him wondering what he had seen and what he thought about it.

Unlike the other two doctors at the hospital, Dr Winters was an arcane. Specifically, he was an Elf. He claimed to be Vanir, a Spring Elf with Elemental Water magic from the Sphere of Springvale. But Mercy suspected that was a lie. She had seen him do magic once, and while the water was moving, she noticed it was being moved by Elemental Wind —it was the wind that sparkled with magic, not the water. It was often very difficult to tell Water from Wind magic, but she had keen vision for magic.

If Dr Winters used Elemental Wind magic, he was most likely a

Winter Elf, an Azir from Winterdom. It was not that Mercy cared what tribe of Elf he was. She knew the Elves were involved in a war, and there might be a good reason for one to hide the true nature of his tribe. Unfortunately, there were also a lot of bad reasons he might be doing so. She found it hard to trust him when she suspected he wasn't honest about such a basic fact. It was one thing to deceive humans. It was too tiresome to try to argue them out of their own disbelief. But why lie to other arcanes?

He smiled at her, a strange knowing smile, as if he were aware of her thoughts. Abruptly, Mercy scrambled to strengthen the shields around her mind. She was able to use psychic magic, which was almost always some mix of dark and light magic. The Azir, the Winter Elves, were said to be very good at telepathy.

"Have a nice day, Mercy," he said. He held open the back door for her. She had the sense that he wanted her to leave. Why? He didn't smoke. He wasn't likely to be here to make a Door like she was.

An unmarked white van entered the parking lot and backed up to deliver something to the service door. Dr Winters walked over to the van, to say something to the men unloading boxes. Odd for a surgeon to be speaking to the delivery guys...

Well, it was none of her business.

She went inside the hospital. Her break had ended five minutes ago, and she was going to be in trouble with her boss.

Seven

July 1, Friday 7:30 am

AFTER HIS MORNING JOG, Miles took a shower at his townhouse and sat on the porch with his coffee. He was looking forward to the daily bicycle ride of the women on the white bike.

Sure enough, at 7:30 on the dot, she came peddling down his road.

That's when he recognized her. The woman from the hospital! Of course. That's where he had seen her before. She was his Lady of the Bicycle. Emboldened by his discovery, he decided to call out to her this morning. When she was in hearing range, he leaned forward.

"Hi there!"

"Hi!" she shouted back.

She had acknowledged his existence. He felt elated. This was already going much better than he had imagined.

By then she was zooming past him. Still, he felt happy. The conversation had not been a total disaster. Whistling to himself, he returned inside and settled down at his desk to get to work on the Herle case.

Eva White handed him another letter from Alephander Guiscard. The Magician had sent a new, identical invitation, without fail every morning. Magician wanted him to hook up with someone to take a job.

Finally, Miles wrote a reply.

To Whom It May Concern,

I'd be happy to discuss doing a job for you, Mr Guiscard, if you leave my love life out of it.

Miles Malone

Miles left the letter on top of the mailbox, but it disappeared before the mail man arrived. He looked everywhere for it, assuming it dropped, he even asked Eva if she took it, but she said no, and also confirmed that the mail man hadn't come by yet.

Aggravated, Miles Malone picked up his phone. He called the Sheriff's office. Cody Lawson answered.

"Hello, Sheriff," Miles said, "I'd like to report a stalker. Someone is sending me letters in such great numbers that I think it constitutes harassment. Can I get an injunction against this person?"

"Who is this?" demanded Sheriff Cody Lawson. "Miles Malone? Is this who I'm speaking with?"

"Yeah, that's me."

"Did the letters contain any threats?"

"No, just a demand to take a job and find a date."

Sheriff Cody's voice became extremely dry. "Are the letters from your mother, Miles?"

"No, they are from Alephander Guiscard."

"The Magician? The internationally famous billionaire celebrity is harassing you? The Magician who owns that big, honking castle on the hill? The Magician who has an army of personal secretaries, a legion of lawyers, and all the employees he needs to do whatever he wants already, so why would he need to offer a job to a nobody like you? *That* Magician?"

"That's what he calls himself. It's not my fault if he's a pretentious prick."

The phone clicked.

Miles laughed to himself and got back to work. If Cody was the one who had informed the Magician about the Dumpster Incident, maybe Cody would also pass on Mile's message to leave him alone.

~

July 1, Friday 16:37 pm

A crack of glass made him snap his head to the door. A moment later five goons in black ninja outfits jumped through the broken French doors and attacked him. They were swathed from head to toe in black cloth, with only their eyes showing. And there was something strange about their eyes: they were huge and extremely bright, as bright as jewels under a hot spotlight.

Five-on-one weren't good odds, but Miles shoved his desk over and leapt behind it, drawing his gun. He shot one of the ninjas in the shoulder, and that one went down, but the others leapt around like acrobats. Nimble as he was, Miles had nothing on these clowns. He did manage to grab the scarf covering the face of one of his assailants. He had a brief vision of snow blue hair, sapphire eyes, tilted eyebrows, and pointy tipped ears.

In movies, enemy ninjas always attacked one after another, giving the hero a chance to beat them up one at a time. Not these ninjas. They were too smart for that, the bastards. They attacked him all at once.

Two of the goons grabbed him by either arm, a third punched him a few times and the one whose face he had uncovered lifted a gun and pointed it at Miles' temple.

Miles was about to say something really witty ("What kind of shoes do ninjas wear? Sneakers?"), in the hopes that his captors would banter back, and he could buy at least a few more moments of life. Unfortunately, these didn't seem to be the sort of goons that engaged in helpful dithering.

The pointy-eared man shot Miles in the head.

~

July 1, Friday 16: 55 pm

That evening on the way home, Mercy thought about the man who had said hello to her in the morning. She wondered if he would still be on his porch. Something about him had perked her curiosity, although she couldn't put her finger on what. It wasn't like her to be intrigued by a random human.

As she passed his home, she heard something. Her ear feathers—her auricle feathers—were extremely sensitive to certain sounds. Sounds that were in the physical mundane realm, and yet not necessarily within human hearing, could be augmented by her magical ears if it reverberated with the psychic energy of someone near death. Her Valkyrie auricle feathers transmitted those sounds to her because, as a reaper, she *needed* to hear them. Traditionally, this was how a Valkyrie located the warrior she was meant to reap on the battlefield. Even in the midst of hundreds of groaning dying warriors, she could home in on the death agony of a single man.

She was hearing the death agony of one man now. She could hear the gargle in his throat, the death rattle of his last breath. Mercy peddled faster and was horrified when her auricle feathers led her to the very townhouse of the man who had waved at her in the morning.

Was it possible that wasn't a coincidence, that somehow the man had experienced a premonition he was going to die and it moved him to signal to the only Valkyrie who could help him? She had a strong sense that he had died in battle. Since there were no battlefields around here, that probably meant he had been fighting criminals while in the pursuit of some kind of law enforcement. Her magic did not distinguish between soldiers and police officers. Even firefighters and other people who saved others would activate her Valkyrie senses of a warrior fighting to protect the innocent. There were limits to how far her abilities extended though. A noble laureate creating a cure in the battle against a disease might be metaphorically a warrior, but he was unlikely to die from violence.

This man, the one she sensed, had been shot. He was definitely a potential client.

However, just as she was about to park her bike and search the building for the victim of a shooting, the sensation of being called dissipated. She could no longer hear the death sound. More than that, she no longer had any connection to a dying spirit at all. It was as if he had been a blip on her radar and now the blip had simply finished.

Mercy had heard rumors and gossip about this phenomenon, but never believed it was real. It was as mythical to reapers as UFOs and Bigfoot were to mundanes. In the reaper community, it was called an UDO.

An Unidentified Dying Object.

The UDO close encounter bothered Mercy so much that she walked her bike for a while, straining her auricle feathers for the sounds of anyone remotely related to her calling.

She had never challenged herself this way before. Perhaps that was why this day, she heard something she had never heard before. It wasn't exactly a death rattle of a warrior. But it was the cough of a man who was dying. She walked toward the mystical sound, trying to get close enough to hear it with her human ears as well.

Her human senses prioritized vision over hearing, so she saw the dying man before she heard him with her human ears. It was a homeless man, probably on his way to the evening meal served at the church by Pastor Mike. But he wasn't going to make it. The Hourglass suspended over his figure showed only a few grains of lifeforce left.

He toppled over and landed in the gutter. Mercy hurried to his side. She laid his head on her lap and stroked his hair, which was matted with mud.

"A reaper will come for you," she telepathed to him, a gentle bridge of her mind directly to his. She knew he was beyond the ability to speak or hear out loud. *"I wish it were me, but I only take warriors."*

"I was a warrior once." He projected an image of himself in uniform, waging in one of the human disputes from decades ago.

"But, if you are a warrior, why don't I sense you?" Mercy telepathed back. *"I should be able to escort your soul to Valhalla."*

A burst of bitterness and hate spewed forth from his mind. He had felt rejected for his effort and thought that his fight was for nothing. He did not feel he had protected anyone or served any honorable cause. Because of that, he had given up not only the people who had sent him into the war, but on *all* people, including himself. And he had given up on fighting for life.

Mercy was able to accept souls filled with great amounts of bitterness and hatred. One reason Warriors went to Valhalla was to fight those dark shadows within themselves. But she couldn't help one who had given up the will to fight at all.

"Please," she whispered to him out loud. "Don't give up. There are still things worth fighting for, ideas worth fighting for, and people worth fighting for. Life is worth fighting for. Don't give up on what is good just because the good sometimes fall on the field of battle. Rise up, defy death, and take up your scythe and shield again. And if you fall, let your body fall, but not your honor."

Telepathically, she showed him all the good moments in his life, the unseen innocents he had saved without having ever met them, and the buddies he had lost along the way who awaited him on the other side.

"Hold on to the Light," she whispered, "Never lose sight of it, though the darkness moves in."

He opened his eyes, wide with wonder. He stared into her face. "Thank you, Angel. I..."

He never finished his last sentence, but he died fighting to say it. That was enough. She reached into his body with the hand of spirit, touched the spirit within him, and took hold of his soul. It was a bright light, a pure sphere of glowing luminance. She threw open a Door and flew through to the other side.

She darted over the floating realms drifting in the empyrean, just as she usually did, but when her feet landed on the ground, she whipped her head about in confusion. Beside her, the glowing soul-ball materialized into a coporeal young man. He also looked confused but only for a moment.

"Eddie!" A young woman cried out. She was also a corporeal, a formally human spirit who had acquired a new body for a stay here in Dayhaven. The young woman ran to Eddie, and she wrapped her arms around him. "I've waited so long for you, I wasn't sure you wanted to be with me."

He kissed her and said, "Of course I did, Betty. But I didn't know how to find you. This angel helped me."

The couple moved away through a beautiful landscape of peaceful ponds full of ducks next to farms that were noisy with chickens and pigs. This was absolutely not Valhalla.

Another being with wings, a Seraph, flew to land beside Mercy. "You are far from your home, Mercy," he said. "Are you supposed to be here?"

"I don't know," she said. "I've never been able to open a Door to any place but Valhalla."

"Perhaps your Calling as a reaper has changed?" suggested the Seraph. "If you wish to switch to bringing souls here, we do not object. Ever since the Guardian of Death disappeared, we have not been receiving those we have Called to us. We are most stressed. Many of them are still lost on earth as wandering ghosts. It is a fate they have not earned."

Mercy blinked, surprised by the offer. "But if I change my home base as a reaper, then I can no longer serve Valhalla."

"That is true," said the Seraph. "But another reaper could take your place there."

"Thank you," said Mercy politely, "but I think I want to stick with what I'm doing now. I'm glad I was able to help this soul at least."

∾

July 1, Friday 8:08

Mercy had to find her way from whatever paradise in Dayhaven she arrived back to Valhalla, in time for dinner. She was trying to get there before sunset, although since it was literally always Day in Dayhaven, that wasn't easy to do. Her human watch stopped working in Dayhaven, because the laws of physics from the Mundane world weren't compatible.

She had to check her back-up timepiece, an angel-made pocket watch, which ran on Light magic. She'd never make it.

Mercy held up her hand, palm up, asking the Light for a small miracle. A cloud of miracles, shaped like shimmering, iridescent butterflies, flitted in the garden, but no one, not even an angel, could force a miracle. A miracle chose you, not the other way around.

Nonetheless, miracles were plentiful in Dayhaven. There were millions of these unclaimed, tiny miracles floating around Dayhaven, gifts created by Protector Angels for their humans which were rejected and sent back. They fluttered around like luminous butterflies, hoping to land on someone and deliver their magic, like pollen to a flower.

One of the gentle miracles landed on Mercy's palm. She felt a wave of calm pour through her. The iridescent flicker of light dissolved into sparkles.

Only seconds later, a Kirin flew to the garden where Mercy stood and landed. Called a Unicorn Dragon, the Kirin, a pearl-white dragon, had a ribbon-slender, a lion's mane of silver light, and a single, golden horn like a lance of sunshine. His eight wings rippled like rainbow dorsal fins.

"Do you need a ride?" asked the Kirin.

"Yes, thank you. To Valhalla."

According to her pocket watch, she arrived exactly on time, at 8:08.

Inside her parents' castle, the banquet table was set for Sebetu, the weekly holiday honoring the creation of the world and the Seven Mortal Spheres. (The Three Eternal Spheres had, of course, preceded the Tree of Worlds itself, although how that worked, since they grew on the Tree, was a metaphysical question that Mercy had never unraveled.) She kissed and hugged her mother, who complained she was late and hastened to introduce Mercy to Hawke Mayers, a recently arrived Warrior.

Mercy's sister and brother, Maven and Merlin, were there, too, and for some reason, Mama hadn't invited blind dates for *them*. Not that there was anything wrong with Hawke. He was gorgeous and, according to his own war stories, a bonafide hero. But Mercy found herself yawning half-way through his fifty-sixth recitation about how he had turned around a battle.

When she could get a word in through the tales of derring-do, Mercy asked her parents and siblings, "Have you ever encountered a UDO?"

A lively discussion ensued, but it boiled down to speculation and rumor, nothing helpful.

Next, Mercy asked about Reapers who changed status.

"Like if I no longer wanted to be a Valkyrie," she said.

"You don't want to be a Valkyrie any longer?" her sister Maven asked.

"Join me over in Takamagahara," suggested Merlin. "It's loads more fun."

Like most males born Valkyries, Merlin had chosen to choose to become a different kind of Reaper. But that was expected, so no one thought twice about it. Mercy knew that for her, it would be different. She was expected to be the heir of a long matrilineal line of Shield-Maiden War Reapers.

"What?" cried Mama. "So, now being a Valkyrie isn't good enough for you? Never mind that I sacrificed so much so that you could have a good career!"

Hawke piped up, "Did I ever tell you about the time I ambushed fifteen of the enemy with only a piece of gum and a stick of dynamite?"

For the first time that evening, Mercy was happy to listen to his story.

Eight

July 2, Saturday

MILES OPENED HIS EYES. He had one hell of a headache.

But that seemed like not much of a price to pay considering he knew he had been shot in the head. This time there was no getting around what had happened. He had been killed. The big sleep. The end of the line. The final bus stop. The big enchilada. He bought the farm.

And yet, here he was. Waking up in his office. Which was a damn mess, by the way. That was one problem with waking up from the dead. You couldn't just leave cleaning up your mistakes to your nearest next of kin.

He removed his shirt and threw it away because it was covered with brains and blood. But when he rubbed his head, it felt whole. He even felt like possibly his hair was a little thicker and curlier than before.

He had no idea how to deal with the fact that he had just apparently healed himself from a direct headshot. So he decided to deal with something that he did understand. Five goons had tried to kill him. They looked like hired guns to him. Professional, but exotic at the same time.

He went over the details of their behavior and appearance. Acrobatic. Check. Weird costumes? Check. Attack that followed right after he insulted the Magician on the phone to the Sheriff, who was apparently the Magician's lap dog? Check.

Miles showered again. Put on clean clothes. Packed his gun. He was going to not learn his lesson. He was going to not leave well enough alone.

He was going to kick over a beehive.

~

Driving up the hill, Miles noted the casino on the right side of three buildings and the hotel was on the left. Visible between those two huge buildings was the fantastic architecture of Arcana Castle, complete with soaring towers and crenelated stone walls. What he thought was the entrance to the Castle proved to be a collection of rooms and a vestibule that led to the Castle. It didn't have was a moat with crocodiles. But he did have to climb a crazy ton of steps to reach the huge portcullis that passed as a front door to this monstrosity.

It was the first time that Miles had been to the Castle itself. He'd done a few jobs for the Magician before, but those had either all been done through correspondence and email or else he had reported to an office in the complex at the hotel and casino.

There was a big metal door knocker with a face that looked like a gargoyle. Because, of course, there was a gargoyle, right? There wasn't anything too cheesy for this guy, Miles thought in disgust.

~

The door opened and a man in a three-piece tailored suit gestured to enter a great hallway.

Miles stared at the man who had welcomed him. He had dark red curly hair, pale skin and bright green eyes, and pointy ears.

"Owen McGee." Miles bared his teeth.

"Welcome to the castle of the Magician, Miles Malone," said Owen. "We've been expecting you."

Miles nodded and strolled into the hallway. He studied the rich surroundings first, then looked again at the man who had welcomed him.

"So you still work for the Magician?" Miles said over a tight smile. "Were you working for the Magician during your adventure with Eleni Bendox when someone knocked me unconscious and left me in a dumpster? Were you working for the Magician when you paid me with fake bills?"

Owen McGee cleared his throat. He managed to look both embarrassed and cocky, regretful and unapologetic at the same time. Like a gambler who lost money on a roll but was going to give it one more try.

"Actually," Owen said, "That was real money, just not used here in this Sphere."

"This Sphere? Do you mean this planet? Are you some kind of alien?"

"No, it's more complicated than that."

"I bet." Miles snorted. "Who the hell uses rainbow money with cartoon characters? Disneyland on Mars?"

"I'm from much further away than Mars, and yet much closer as well," declared Owen.

Miles glared at him. "If I had met you anywhere else, I would have started this conversation by punching you in the face. But I'm trying to be civilized here. I am here by invitation, and I want to see Alephander Guiscard."

"I will show you to the office where he's waiting to see you. I really am sorry you were attacked while trying to help Eleni and me. I'll pay you back when I get the money. I have a new job, so it should be soon."

Miles heard a disturbing echo with his own refrain. "Don't bother," he said. "I wouldn't trust you not to give me counterfeit."

"Then perhaps you would accept payment from me," said a cultured female voice, an alto rather than soprano, but musical and educated. She was coming down the hall to meet him as well, but she strolled at a more decorous pace than the springy Owen McGee.

Miles recognized Eleni Bendox. The last time he had seen her, she had looked disheveled and frightened. Now she looked fully put together again, the consummate legal professional. She was dark skinned enough to be African, rather than African-American, but she had no accent. Her hair was expertly braided in dozens of long, tiny braids that terminated in a dozen beads carved from semi-precious stones. She had so many braids in fact, that her hair piled in layers on both sides of her head and down the back of her neck. The effect was somewhat Egyptian, as if her hair were also a headdress or crown. She wore a white business suit with a pencil skirt and matching heels. And even though they were indoors, she wore white-framed mirrored sunglasses.

She reached Miles and held out her hand. He shook it, now quite confused about what was going on.

"Please don't tell me you also work for the Magician." Miles grimaced. "I thought you work for the Attorney General's office."

"It's a small town, Mr Malone. I do both."

"Doesn't that involve you in a conflict of interest?"

"Indeed, there are some cases from which I must recuse myself. For instance, the unfortunate events that involve you. I can understand why you blamed Mr McGee, but he was actually as much a victim of the villainous plot as myself. We managed to extricate ourselves from the difficulties and apprehend the criminals responsible with the help of Mr Guiscard."

"Glad to hear that," said Miles. "The Magician sounds like a real nice guy."

Underneath the sunglasses, her eyebrow peeked out as it lifted over her eyes. "'*Nice*,'" she echoed, "is not the word I would use. Up until recently, I would not even have been certain whether I could call him good. But people can change for the better."

"In my experience," drawled Miles, "when people change, it's usually for the worse."

"Is that so? Does that also apply to the recent changes in your own life?"

"What recent changes would those be?" he countered.

"You can't bullshit a bullshitter," said Owen McGee. "We both saw you die. It ain't natural to come back from the dead. You're not natural, Mr. Malone. You're a bloody freak."

Miles felt a cold stone slide right down his throat into his belly at the words that reflected exactly what he himself had been thinking since he woke up in the dumpster.

"Owen," said Eleni reprovingly. "Don't tease."

"That's me, full of magic tricks," Miles joked, to hide his discomfort. "I'm a regular magician, just like your boss. You know, I performed magic for a mime, once. He was speechless."

"Please follow us, Mr Malone," said Eleni. "The Magician will explain everything you need to know."

$\sim$

June 2, Saturday

If the long walk through the Castle filled with amazing works of art, velvet wallpapered and hardwood paneled rooms, with double story ceilings and illuminated by precious Tiffany chandeliers was supposed to intimidate Miles Malone with the Magician's opulent wealth and taste, Miles had to admit it was working. He had only seen places like this on television. He had to pinch himself to remind himself that all of this was owned by one man. One very eccentric and enigmatic man, whose goals were unknown to him. With resources like this, what kind of 'magic tricks' could the Magician pull off?

They brought him to a library about the size of a football field, lined with three stories of books on one side. Sofas and recliners circled a riverstone fireplace at one end of the room. The last wall, running the length of the library was all glass, three stories of glass that looked out over gardens and marble pavilions in the foreground, and Arcana Lake and the white-capped peaks of the Rockies in the distance. It was a breathtaking view.

There was a long, engraved table inlaid with semi-precious stone mosaics. Mr. McGee and Ms Bendox showed Mr. Malone to a seat. There were already stacks of paper sitting on the table. What is this?

The lawyer, Eleni Bendox, took charge, seating herself across from Miles. "This is the paperwork you will need to sign if you wish to accept the Magician's offer of employment. It includes a non-disclosure agreement, standard terms, as well as some more detailed explanations of your responsibilities. Did you bring a companion with you today?"

"No, somehow, I forgot that," Miles said sarcastically. "Perhaps I wish to hear first what kind of job requires me to be married. Is it even legal for you to demand that? Maybe I'll sue."

The lawyer looked alarmed at that. Probably that seemed like a real possibility to her, although the last thing Miles intended was to meet the Magician in a court of law, which was undoubtedly Guiscard's playing field, among others. No way would Miles be able to fight him there and win. He just liked to poke and see what response he got. Miles pushed the stack of papers back toward the lawyer.

"I have no intention of signing a dang thing until I hear more about what the job actually involves."

"Unfortunately, we can't tell you about the job until you sign the papers."

"Is the Magician going to meet with me or just you two?"

McGee and Bendox exchanged a look. A long pause followed. On an unseen cue, both rose simultaneously and left the room.

A few moments later, Alephander Guiscard walked in. Even in his own house, he wore his costume: a white tuxedo with a long, red-lined cape and a top hat. Miles had seen pictures of him wearing black silk, but this outfit was all white, except for the red lining. Was the Magician trying to indicate that he had gone from being a black hat to a white hat? Not very subtle. Besides it was going to take more than a change of costume to sway Miles.

Miles had taken a chair facing the large windows, and rather than sit with his back to the window, the Magician sat down at the head of the table. This put several empty chairs between them, which suited Miles fine. He didn't want to be within striking distance of this guy.

"You didn't sign the papers," the Magician growled. "There's nothing I can tell you right now. Also, you need a woman."

"'You need a woman.'" Miles mimicked the Magicians deep voice mockingly. "That's a pretty bizarre request, Mister."

The Magician shrugged. "Someone you are in love with. It could be a man, if you prefer."

"I didn't come here to discuss my love life, and I didn't come here to discuss my work. I came here to ask you—what is your beef with me? Why did you send your goons to try to kill me?"

"Explain why you think I sent anyone to kill you."

"Who else would send guys dressed up to look like Elves? Or were they supposed to be Vulcans? I get my pointy-eared races mixed up."

The Magician leaned forward, suddenly intent and interested. He acted like a man who was surprised and alarmed, although it was difficult to tell. Everything he did was an act, Miles reminded himself. Guiscard was literally an actor.

"What color hair did the Elves have?" the Magician asked.

"Really? Do you want to make sure they got the costume right? They had blue hair and they were dressed like ninjas. All in black."

"Were their clothes black or very dark purple?"

"What am I, Pantone? They shot me and then everything went black. They shot me in the head. Then I woke up."

"That you did." The Magician leaned back, cool again. "Don't you find that a little unusual?"

"At first, I did, but now that I've seen McGee and the lady lawyer here, I'm beginning to realize it might be your recruiting style. Both of them said they were kidnapped and traumatized. Then 'magically',"— Miles imbued the word with a lot of sarcasm— "They suddenly attribute their rescue to you. And now they're working for you. After having signed mysterious non-disclosure agreements. You deal in tricks and deception, illusion, and misdirection. You set up the attacks on me to make me think I died and came back to life."

"You think all of that is a trick."

"Occam's razor. Are you familiar with the concept?"

"I see your Occam and raise you Einstein: 'An explanation should be as simple as possible'," said the Magician. "'But not simpler.' You have a bias which allows you to keep your current view of the universe. I congratulate you for coming up with a particularly creative approach. I have no need to be the one to convince you that your theory is wrong. When more facts accumulate that you cannot account for, you will find your current theory is too simple. Besides, you obviously have not met your counterpart yet. You cannot take the job until you have a life partner."

"Look, Magician, let me be frank with you about my love life..." Miles leaned forward to confess. "Five years ago, I asked my childhood best friend—the most beautiful woman in the world—my girlfriend—to marry me. And all three said no."

Alephander's lip twitched.

"Aha! I saw that! You almost laughed!" Miles accused.

"You're single and you need to have a partner," said Alephander Guiscard.

"I'm not dragging a lady into this."

Alephander's lips twitched again. "You may find that she is the one who drags you. There is an ongoing debate among people of my profession, which of us has the strongest magic. I would have said that was me, and yet arguably, the magic of love is greater than that. Even I was unable to resist."

Miles crossed his arms. "When you say 'your profession', you mean Stage Magicians?"

"I mean wizards," the Magician said matter-of-factly. "Wielders of real magic, not fake magic. Specifically, I am a Guardian of the Gates between the Spheres. The ancient word is *Sarmat*. I am telling you this even though you have not yet signed the papers, because I know you do not yet believe me."

"And if I told anyone else, they wouldn't believe me either," said Miles.

"Correct." The Magician smiled wolfishly at him. "But if you are not willing to switch jobs, perhaps you would still be willing to let me hire you one more time in your current profession. You are a detective, Mr. Malone."

The Magician snapped his fingers. A stack of folders appeared in his hand. Miles didn't know where the stuff came from, but that was a standard stage magic trick, so Miles wasn't at all impressed.

The Magician handed him the stack of papers.

"More stuff for me to sign?" asked Miles.

"Not exactly."

Nine

July 2, Saturday

MERCY DIDN'T RETURN to the Mundane Sphere until after sunset on Saturday. After spending a day with her parents and traveling between the Spheres, Mercy was always tired and craved sweets. She debated whether it was worth it to stop at the store, which was a lot of work in her current state of exhaustion. She had just decided to go straight home when she remembered her empty fridge. Finally, the need for ice cream won. She stopped at the market and bought way too much food. Then she had to balance two of the bags on the handlebars, one on the left and one on the right, because she had bought more groceries than could fit in the basket behind her seat.

She peddled home slowly because of the extra weight.

There was a strange glow following her. She paused her bike and put one foot down on the pavement to look back over her shoulder. There was a ghost very close to her and several more trailing behind.

"Uh...Are you all veterans?" she asked.

"No," admitted the closest ghost. The other ghosts also echoed sadly, "Noooooo..."

"You're going to have to find your own reapers," she told them. "I can't help you."

She started cycling again. This time, she didn't stop until she reached her apartment.

She locked her bike up outside and tried to carry as many groceries as she could all at once, sliding the handles of several bags onto each of her arms. Fortunately, despite her plump and rather weak-looking human appearance, she had the strength of a Valkyrie even in this form. She was able to *carry* all the bags; it was just a matter of *balancing* them. She couldn't help but notice that there was now a whole throng of ghosts crowding around her.

"Are *any* of you veterans?" she asked. "Did you ever serve in the police or fire department or... Anything close? Were you at least killed by violence?"

A ghost with an ax through its head pressed close to her. "I was killed by violence," the ghost said eagerly.

Mercy placed her hand inside the ghost spirit and saw a vision of an angry wife.

"You beat your wife until she got angry enough to kill you in self-defense," Mercy complained. "That's not an honorable death in battle, I'm sorry. I can't help you."

She had a feeling that if the ghost knew where it was likely to end up on the other side, he wouldn't be so eager to crossover either.

But many of the other ghosts had not died from any sin or misunderstanding that should've condemned them to stay trapped on the Mundane Sphere. They were spirits that would have normally been passed through their Doors by their respective reapers. For some reason, so many ghosts were trapped on earth these days. Some people who knew exactly where they were headed after death. Those people could get through the Door on their own without help. But many other spirits could not.

"Please, please," begged the ghosts. "We saw you help the other man. He wasn't one of yours, but you found his Door."

That was true, but Mercy still thought that was a fluke. Also, she didn't want to lose her connection to Valhalla by opening the Door for a new genre of ghost. If she did that too many times, she would get permanently reassigned. Her mother would think Mercy was rejecting her Valkyrie heritage and be heartbroken.

But the misery of the ghosts tore at her heart, and she decided to at least try. She picked one that seemed the most likely candidate and put her hand into his core and then tried to summon a Door.

At first it looked promising. A Door, although a very small Door, like the door of a shed or something, appeared in the air. The ghost flew to it and Mercy try to pull it open. But it was locked. She pounded on it, she rattled the door handle, she even tried to change into her Valkyrie form and kick it open, but nothing worked. The ghost screamed in frustration.

"Are you locking me out?" demanded the ghost. "Why would you do this to me?"

"You hate us," another ghost accused her. "You're doing it on purpose. You want us to suffer!"

"She's an unfaithful little bitch!" shouted the ghost with the ax in his head.

He reached out and scattered all of her groceries. He was more than a ghost. He was a poltergeist. That wasn't a good thing.

"Now, see here!" Mercy shouted back. "You of all people have no right to start pointing fingers!"

But now all of the ghosts, even the milder ones, were riled up by the more violent poltergeists. The regular ghosts couldn't touch Mercy if she didn't want them to make contact with her, but poltergeists had the ability to materialize themselves briefly into physical form and hit and kick. They were also able to lift up the fallen food items nearby and hurl the butter, frozen crescents and tub of ice-cream at her head.

She whipped herself back into Valkyrie form to fight them, but she was handicapped by the fact that she didn't really want to hurt them, even though it now seemed the ghosts were determined to drag her into their ranks.

∼

July 2, Saturday Night

Mercy was still standing in the street in front of her apartment building. A few cars passed by and there was some pedestrian traffic, but only mundanes. They looked at her like she was a crazy woman. Mundanes couldn't see her Valkyrie form and they couldn't see the ghosts, so all they saw was a woman waving her hands at the air and shouting at nothing.

Then an arcane, a young woman about Mercy's age, did a double take when she passed by. It was clear she could not only see Mercy's true form, which any arcane could have done, but she could also see the ghosts themselves. That meant she had spirit magic, the rarer form of magic.

In her human form, the young woman wore a Japanese school uniform—a Cosplay version, since she was no mortal schoolgirl. She was, however, even shorter than Mercy. Then she switched to her other form. She was still quite petite and beautiful, but now there was an eerie edge to her appearance that probably would've scared any mundane who saw her. Her long white dress was drenched in blood. Her eyes blazed fiery red. Her bone white hair billowed behind her. The three-inch black talons on both her hands and her vulture feet were also creepy. She was a Shinigami, but obviously a very young one, probably less than a century old.

The girl ran to the throng of ghosts and shouted at them, "Hey! Leave her the hell alone!"

The Shinigami pulled out a automatic rifle and started shooting at the ghosts. The rifle was glowing faintly, showing that it was a spirit weapon and had no physical existence, so no mundanes would stop her for shooting randomly into the air with an automatic weapon.

The ghosts scattered, except for the one with the hatchet in his head. He also tried to run, but the new arrival put away her gun and took out a lasso that glowed blood red. She used this to throw around him and hogtie him on the ground like a cowboy with a horse rustler. Then she pulled out a dagger made out of bones, which was already dipping dripping with blood, and drew a circle in the dirt. A black cavernous pit, lined with sharp teeth, yawned open where the circle had been. Deep within the hole, a dull red glow burned, as if of some fire seethed far below. The ghost with the hatchet in his head fought wildly but the red-eyed girl smacked him and kicked him and finally shoved him into the hole. It snapped shut like a toothy mouth, licked the dirt rim with a snake tongue, like someone smacking their lips after a tasty bite, and even burped. Then the dirt settled back into being nothing more than dirt again.

"Wow!" Mercy exclaimed. "That was amazing. I guess I must be out of shape. It's been a while since I had to fight the spirits I came to reap."

Usually, Mercy's clients welcomed her. But as a Valkyrie, she was equipped to go to fend off evil spirits and defend good ones. It had been a while since she had practiced her fighting skills. In fact, she thought guiltily, not since she moved to earth. She eyed the other woman speculatively, wondering if she could talk the Shinigami into becoming a sparring partner.

"I didn't know there was another reaper living in Arcana Glen," Mercy babbled on happily. "Did you just move here?"

"I'm only here for the reapers conference. I came a little early so I could sightsee a little bit in America. I live in Tokyo."

"Were you born and raised on earth?"

"Yes. It's a long story." The woman sighed.

"It usually is," said Mercy. "But it makes it easier in some ways. When I accepted my first placement as a reaper, it wasn't my first visit to the Mundane Sphere, so at least I didn't have to learn everything at once. But I've been so overwhelmed lately! Well, I guess you could tell that." Mercy laughed. "If you need a local to show you around, I'd be glad to do so."

"Thank you," said the girl. "You're from Dayhaven, aren't you? You don't mind that I'm from the other side? I know the conference will include all kinds of reapers, but I wasn't sure anyone from your side would want to socialize with me outside of that."

"We each have jobs to do, no wrong in that. As long as you're not taking any soul ahead of his time." Mercy chuckled.

The other reaper did not laugh. "I've had the opposite problem. Too many evil souls have been escaping me lately. This one that I just reaped, I have been chasing a long time. I never expected to find him here. Why were all the ghosts attacking you? And by the way, you didn't seem out of shape to me. You were fighting magnificently, but there were so many of them. I think you'd find it easier to even the odds if you used a gun."

"I've never had something like that happened to me before. Is it just me, or is the ghost problem getting worse?"

"It's a problem for all reapers," said the girl.

"My name is Mercy Wise." She held out her hand.

"Sumiko Sadukatzu," said the Shinigami.

Ten

July 2, Saturday Night

MILES OPENED the first folder and saw a photo and a typed-up page almost like a police report of background information. The next folder contained another photo and a more detailed biography. There were twenty-one in all.

"What are these?" he asked the Magician. "Who are these people?"

"Those were my former colleagues, fellow members of a certain council. The Council of Guardians.

"So ...magic wizards."

The Magician inclined his head. "Even if you do not believe their profession is real, you can look them up and you will find they are real people. They were all murdered. I am seeking to find the killer."

Miles flipped through the pages of photos and biographical descriptions more carefully. Olly Grey the Fool. A man with a goofy expression and a broken nose. Raphael, a "Fabio" look-alike who wore a bathrobe and... wings? Sabriel Izbognir. An astonishingly beautiful woman with dark black hair and dark eyes. No... when Miles perused the photo carefully, he realized she had dark *purple* hair and matching *purple* eyes. And she had pointy ears.

The death date on every paper was the same.

"They all died on the same day."

"Yes. Sitting in the same room. They were killed by magic, something you do not yet believe in. Perhaps it would be easier for you to understand if you talked to my resident scientist. He was as skeptical of magic as you, even though like you he had experienced it personally. However, he prefers to describe it as alternate forms of physics found in parallel dimensions of the multi-verse. Does that explanation make more sense to you?"

"Not really." Miles shrugged. "All you've done is replace traditional magic terms with science-fiction gobbledygook."

"If he showed you the mathematical formulas associated with this alternate form of physics, would that help you?"

"I'm good at math when it comes to things like calculating the odds I'll never win the lottery and doing my own taxes," said Miles. "But any math used for physics involving dimensions and multi-verses is going to be way over my head. So, no, that's no help to me. Again, I would just have to take your word for it."

"But you are the kind of man who has to discover evidence for himself," said the Magician. "We are not as different as you think Mr Malone."

Miles tried to figure out if that was supposed to be a compliment or an insult.

"I don't expect you to be able to solve these murders by yourself," said the Magician. "But if you can even provide a key piece of information to me, anything to advance our case, I am willing to pay you handsomely."

He named a price. It was about what Miles made in a year. More than enough to pay his mortgage and his secretary; enough that he wondered if he should reject it as a bribe.

"How is it a bribe to pay you to do the job you do already professionally?" The Magician demanded impatiently. "Now you're just making excuses."

"Are you reading my thoughts?" Miles demanded.

"How could I do that unless I was a telepath?" asked the Magician. "Surely that falls under the sort of magic in which you don't believe."

Was telepathy magic? Before today, Miles would have definitely said yes. But now he was beginning to wonder if maybe there were a few things that should be moved from the category of impossible to possible.

"If anyone had telepathy, it would be a guy like you," grumbled Miles.

"Very astute. Telepathy is a form of psychic magic. Psychic magic is one of nine forms of magic that exist. The reason that magics seem unnatural to you as a human being, is that the nine forms of magic are 'unnatural' in this Mundane Sphere."

"I heard that term before. Why do you call it a sphere? Isn't that a synonym for a planet?"

"In this case, it is closer to a alternate universe or a alternate dimension. Again, the scientist could give you the precise mathematical explanation. I use the traditional alchemical term, archaic as it may be. Here is the point. I believe you are able to see what magics people possess, to evaluate their abilities and intensities. The culprit who murdered these people was able to wield all nine forms of magic. I want you to make me a list of who has all nine forms of magic."

"I don't even know what the nine forms are," said Miles. "And I don't socialize with wizards. Wouldn't you be better suited to make that list yourself?"

"Of course I have tried. But I am too close to the problem. Whoever the murderer is knows that I am investigating and knows that I am a threat to him. He has no doubt crafted his entire strategy to deceive me. I, myself, have all nine forms of magic, and I pride myself on being able to determine who else is my equal. But, there are ways of hiding one's magic. It is easy to have a skill and yet not use it in front of others. I will give you an example. My third wife."

"Your third wife was a wizard?" Miles tried not to smirk. "So it includes women too. Oh, of course it does. There were women in the photos you gave me. Therefore, it's not just wizards but wizardesses we should be looking for..."

Miles trailed off because he realized he was already talking as if he were planning to take on this case.

"I haven't agreed to anything yet," he said hastily. "But don't let me stop you from telling me how your ex-wife tricked you. Mine just slept with her boss and told me she was working overtime. Simple and classic. I still fell for it. So, yeah, I know all about being too close to a problem."

"Indeed," said the Magician. "I thought my third wife was mundane. That means, a person completely without any magic from another Sphere. If you have some magic, you are called an arcane; and those who have a great deal of power in one area are what I have called wizards. I used every power I possess to screen this woman for magic and detected nothing. However, her magic was unique. She was a changeling. A changeling is someone who can take on the appearance of someone else, but usually they don't also get the target's magic. This changing was more powerful than most. When she became someone, she became them in every way, including whatever powers they possessed or failed to possess. When she took the form of a human, she was indistinguishable from a human, seemingly without magic. And yet she could change back into a magic user whenever she wanted by taking on someone else's form. She infiltrated my house disguised as someone without any powers. Fortunately, she was not able to imitate me, so I was able to stop her from robbing me. But I was not able to keep her imprisoned. She escaped and is still at large."

"So..." murmured Miles, "...and I'm just indulging you here, please understand... by the laws you've been telling me about, the laws of your weird multi-dimensional magical universe, someone like that could have all nine forms of power because she could imitate nine different people, each of which has only one power, but by switching between them she'd have more."

"Exactly.

"So why isn't she a suspect?"

"She is. As am I. However, I have been investigated and cleared of the charges. I was not the killer."

"Sheriff Cody cleared you of all charges, huh?" snickered Miles. "Or was it Eleni Bendox, who also works for you, or Judge Renaci? That guy looks suspiciously like a guy who tried to kill me."

"It was a quorum of Angels."

"What! Now you're going to tell me angels and demons exist too?

Look, you can have your wizards and else or you can have your angels and demons, but you can't have both!"

"Why would you assume they are incompatible? They are from different Spheres."

"I think you're just getting greedy now."

"Listen, detective. I'm going to challenge you to do something. I want you to go to the Fourth of July celebration at the park. It will be held in two days. I want you to take a date. You don't have to introduce her to me, if you think I am such a danger to females." The Magician smirked, as if he didn't mind being a certain kind of danger to females. "Before you ask, magic operates on all levels, spiritual, psychic, and physical. Something about having a companion can enhance magic. I realize that you don't know who you are ultimately meant to be with yet, but indulge me and at least try to find a date."

"That's the challenge? Take a date to the Fourth of July celebration? I am really at a loss to see how this is going to help solve a mass murder."

"I expect you will be experiencing an acceleration of your abilities. I think you will start seeing things that you may mistake for hallucinations at first. Lights and patterns. I can't tell you the exact form the visions will take for you, because these kinds of things are idiosyncratic. I know the general outline but not the specifics, which will be unique to the way your soul interprets the Calling from the Light."

"The Calling from the... Come on you don't mean..."

"I am not here to debate semantics with you. You know what I mean by 'the highest power.' Again, your particular vision or name is not important to me, it reflects your own personal and cultural background. The point is, I think you will start to see the people of Arcana Glenn in a way you have never seen them before. I want to tell you that it is not a sign you are losing your grip on reality. It is a step towards being able to perceive a part of reality which until now has been closed to you."

"Or it's another trick of yours. And now you are priming me to interpret it the way you want me to. Why don't you prove your power is real?"

Alephander Guiscard steepled his fingers. "It's dangerous to taunt a wizard to prove his power, detective. What is it you want?"

"A court order to the Veteran's Hospital here in Arcana Glen to release their medical records to me for another case I'm working on. Pull that off, and I'll believe in magic."

Alephander Guiscard regarded Miles in silence.

"Of course, if you can't do it..." Miles shrugged his shoulders, leaned back, interlocked his fingers behind his head. "I'll know you're not the real Santa, just a nice man with a beard."

"You are a very stubborn man, Mr Malone. I only hope you will eventually apply that stubbornness to helping me find justice for the friends and colleagues I lost on the day of the massacre."

July 2, Saturday Night

Miles lived over his office, so when he arrived home that night, he noticed a large, officious white envelope had been slid under the front door. Curious, he opened it.

It was a court order to the Veteran's Hospital, bidding them to release any and all records requested by Miles Malone. It was time-stamped exactly one hour after Miles had issued his challenge to Alephander Guiscard.

Dang.

Maybe the man really was a Magician.

July 3, Sunday Morning

Mercy found the man with the Infinity Hourglass in his aura waiting for her for by the bicycle rack. Her heart started pumping again. By the Light, he was fine looking. What was she supposed to do in the presence of a man who made her tongue do two backflips instead of doing its job to help her speak?

"Are you here to ask more questions of the hospital staff?" she asked.

"Uh..." He scuffed one foot against the other, glanced down and then looked up at her with a hopeful, somewhat bashful smile. It was totally adorable and sexy at the same time. "...yes." He waved a large envelope. "I have a court order this time."

She blinked. "How nice."

Miles tilted his head to stare at the sky, then scratched behind his ear. "I was hoping I would also run into you. I hope you won't think I'm stalking you. I knew you worked here, and I recognized your bicycle. I just wanted to talk to you, but if you're not interested, I'll leave you alone."

"My... bicycle?"

"Yeah, remember I waved at you the other morning?" He smiled hopefully.

Mercy teetered back on her heels, emitting a gasp of shock. She was so surprised, she almost shifted into her Valkyrie form.

"You... you're the man who waved at me?"

He nodded.

Mercy bit her lip to keep from exclaiming, *No wonder my Death-sense lost track of you. You didn't die!*

But how was that possible?

She couldn't very well ask him that. Desperately, she cast about for some other reason to keep talking to him. She was too shy to suggest what she really wanted, to go out for drinks or dinner, but she remembered what Bev said he had been asking about.

"Uh... why not come back inside and we could discuss the case you are interested in. Are you asking about poor Gawain Herle's death?"

"You heard I was investigating that?" he asked.

"It's a small town and an even smaller hospital. Rumors travel very quickly here."

"I can see that."

She walked inside with him. She told him the facts of Gawain's case as clearly as she could.

"So you were surprised he died?" Miles asked.

"Very surprised."

"Did you know him well?"

"I knew he was a good man. He seemed healthy."

"Did anyone else think it was strange?"

Mercy hesitated.

"Don't worry, if it's just rumors or feelings, I'll take it with a grain of salt," promised Miles, "So don't be afraid to report anything odd, no matter how unimportant it seems."

"Well, Dr Cornel was also upset. He said, 'if I'd known, I'd have used a jewel.'"

"I don't understand."

Mercy started to explain, then snapped her jaw shut. She had a suspicion that Cornel meant magic. But she had no proof. Also, it made no sense. Some Stone Witches were able to heal people by channeling Light magic via special crystals. They could strengthen the spirit itself by an infusion of Light. Cornel seemed to know magic was real; he was Sensitive to it, aware when it was used around him, although he was too discreet to admit as much openly. But he wasn't a Stone Witch, or any kind of arcane. Even if he had a proper Healing Crystal, he couldn't channel Light through it.

Nor could she explain all of this to Miles Malone, a human.

"You'll have to ask Cornel himself," said Mercy. "If you can get the records, you should also look into two other cases, Miguel Ramos and Tony Ban." She spelled their full names for him.

"I will, thanks for the tip."

She wished to prolong her time with him, but what else was there to say?

"Mercy..." He twisted his whole body away as if incredibly embarrassed and then visibly forced himself to face her and take a deep breath. "I was wondering if you would go with me to the Fourth of July celebration? There are fireworks in the park."

"Like... On a date?"

"Yeah. Like that."

"Oh my. No one has invited me on a date to a social event in the park since I was in High School."

He winced. "Okay, this was obviously a stupid idea..."

"No! I love it. I would love to go. I never expected you to... Well, I didn't think a guy like you would be interested in someone like me." Mercy flushed.

"Someone like you? You mean an incredibly beautiful, talented, and compassionate woman? What male with a pulse would not be interested?"

She blushed to the roots of her hair.

"My names is Miles Malone, by the way," he said.

"I'm Mercy Wise."

"I know." He hurried to add, "Your friend Beverly told me. Because I asked. So, can I pick you up at 18:00... uh, six o'clock..."

"On what day?" she asked.

"The Fourth of July is usually held on the fourth. Of July."

Now she covered her face with her hands. "I'm making an idiot of myself."

"No, not at all. You can't imagine how nervous I was. I haven't been this nervous since I asked Lindsey Olsen out on a date for High School." He grinned at her. "I can pick you up at six and..."

"All the traffic will be terrible. I know where you live. I can meet you there and we can just walk over. I'll bike to your townhouse, but is it okay if I leave my bike there?"

"There are no racks that I've seen, but you can store it in my office. Actually, in my secretary's office. So... It's a date then."

"It's a date."

They stood there without saying anything but unable to move away. Mercy was aware of her physical attraction but also of something more. She could still see the odd infinity-shaped Hourglass superimposed over his body, but for the first time she realized it was not static. It was spinning, slowly, so that it did rotate to an upright position eventually, but then tipped down to the other side, became completely horizontal for a while and kept turning until it had completely reversed itself and was upside down from its former position. Like hands on the clock, it kept going around and around.

She couldn't understand what it was about his strange energy that pulled her like a magnet. Was it good or bad that she experienced this magical connection at the level of spirit in addition to their physical connection? Was it a sign that they were fated to be together, or was it an indication that he was using his power to influence her for some ulterior purpose?

Eleven

July 4, Monday Evening

MILES WAS glad he had taken the advice to leave the car behind. The crowds increased the closer they got to the park. There were many families, and everyone was dressed up in red, white, and blue. Earlier in the day there had been a parade down main street. Different city clubs and all of the school children, who were in dance teams or martial arts teams, participated by building pickup-truck floats or decorating their bikes. It wasn't something he had checked out this year, but he could imagine participating in future years if he had kids and actually integrated into the community.

Now, where had that crazy thought come from? The Magician really did have some kind of magic if he had gotten Miles thinking about marriage and kids. When it came to relationships, Miles was once bitten, twice shy. He had figured he'd probably settle into a curmudgeonly Old-Manship, and spend his golden years shouting at kids to get off his lawn.

But as soon as Mercy arrived, all smiles and curves and girl-next-door enticement, he felt those same fantasies drifting back. Buying a house together, tying the knot, a whole yard full of little Miles and little

Mercies... *Stop that right now,* he told himself. *You'll be lucky if you can talk her into bed, never mind into buying a house with you.*

Even Mercy had dressed up for the festive occasion, with a white T-shirt with red polka dots and blue jeans. Miles was wearing jeans as well, and a dark blue shirt so he supposed he would at least not clash with everyone.

"Is this a childhood tradition for you?" he asked.

"The Fourth of July in general or the celebration here in Arcana Glen?" asked Mercy. "I didn't actually move to Arcana Glen until I took the nursing job at the Veteran's Hospital. But I used to visit my grandparents every summer, and they always celebrated the Fourth of July."

He was about to make a comment when he noticed something floating in front of her. It wasn't exactly physically there. He rubbed his eyes, just like characters did on television when they thought they were hallucinating. He finally understood the motive for doing that. He could definitely see something, even though he was certain it was not physically in front of him. It was like those little floaty snakes you sometime see after looking at a bright light, or a moat in your eye, or an eyelash. Naturally, his first instinct was to try to clear his eyes and make sure there was nothing physically wrong with his vision.

His eyes were fine; the image did not go away. It remained, faint and ghostly, but glowing, like a holograph. The more closely he studied the vision the more it seemed integrated into the rest of what he saw, although he was still quite certain he was the only one who could see it.

When he looked at Mercy, he saw lights forming a line that ran right down the center of her body. It was as if someone were shining spotlights on her, or perhaps as if several glowing light bulbs had turned on inside her. The lights—at first—were simply fuzzy balls of color. The one the top was pure white, the next light was purple, then blue, green and so on, down the rainbow. The glow right between her legs was hot crimson and thinking about it too much made him start to adjust his pants. He dragged his eyes to the green light right over her heart.

The lights were not simply spotlights, he realized, but complicated glyphs created from interlocking geometric shapes. A circle inscribed with a triangle or a square or a more complicated polygon, and within each facet, these geometric shapes were labeled with little numbers. A large number was in the middle of the circle of color.

Mercy cleared her throat. Miles realized he had been apparently staring at her breasts for the past several minutes.

"You look fantastic," he said to cover his faux pas.

July 4, Monday Evening

They reached the park, bought tickets at the concession stand to see the fireworks, and entered the large grassy area.

"Oh dear..." said Mercy, "I didn't bring a blanket or chairs."

Miles gestured to the large carry-all he had slung over his shoulder. "I bought us a blanket. But I see that some people went so far as to pack their own food."

"There's food at the concession stand so that shouldn't be a problem. Let's grab a nice spot before the center of the field is taken up!"

They wound their way through the blankets that had already been staked out like little kingdoms across the field. Everywhere he looked, as soon as Miles concentrated in a certain way, he could see the lights running down the core of every single person. It was like a traffic light, except with seven circles instead of three. Everyone had the entire set of seven circles, but only some people had the lights turned on. The traffic light analogy also fit, because, at first, he only saw people with one light turned on at a time, and that was not counting those who seem to be completely "off."

The more he concentrated, and the more practice he had seeing the lights, the crisper and clear the images became. He perceived the different shapes and different intensities in the light. When he spread out the blanket, and he and Mercy sat down next to each other, he studied her surreptitiously.

Now that he was alerted to the fact that some people could have their traffic lights turned on or turned off, this time he was no longer tempted to stare at her breasts, round and tempting as they were, because the light was not strongest in the green spot over her heart.

Mercy was the first person he saw who had *two* lights turned on. One was near her throat, and it was bright blue. The other crowned the top of her head, like a halo, and it was pure white.

When he chose not to focus on the lights, they didn't completely go away but they no longer distracted him from the physical appearance of a person, for instance, this gorgeous woman sitting next to him, threading her fingers and smiling nervously. No doubt she was wondering why he was staring at her in such a bizarre fashion.

They turned the conversation to mundane matters and discussed their lives. He was tickled to find out that Mercy had grown up in Denver, as well as some foreign country that she was a little vague about, but sounded like Norway.

The conversation took an unexpectedly deep turn when they started talking about previous relationships.

"I've never been to the stage where I've considered moving in with a man, never mind marrying him," Mercy said. "I feel like I would need someone to accept me for who I really am first, and that's hard."

"Do you have some deep dark secret I should know about?" Miles teased.

She laughed, but he noticed that she did not actually say no.

"My marriage broke up because my wife cheated on me," he confessed. "But the truth is, I knew I was the one who withdrew from the relationship first, even before the divorce. I let a wall grow between us, a wall of silence. We just stop talking to each other. We stopped sharing things. I threw myself into my work, and I thought she was doing the same. Although I knew things weren't going well, I thought we were doing okay living parallel lives. When I confronted her with her infidelity, she threw it back at me. She told me that being married to me was worse than living alone."

He grimaced. "So now you know, I don't exactly make the best husband material. You've been warned."

"So you agree with me," Mercy countered, "that a relationship can't work unless both people share what's really going on in their lives."

"Yeah," he said. "Ironically what I learned from having my trust broken was realizing that I had never really trusted her in the first place."

Mercy started to say something. Suddenly she looked away. Her expression grew sad and strange. "Trust is hard. I find it very hard to open up, because I fear embarrassing myself. When I was little, I used to wonder what would be worse: to be embarrassed in front of my friends or being beaten to death by snakes. Or falling off the roof. Or getting trapped in a pit and crushed by rocks."

"You were a morbid little girl, weren't you?" He grinned. "I like that."

"I always felt like embarrassment was worse than death."

"Do you know what I've observed?" he asked her. "The things people are most embarrassed about are usually not weaknesses but the things that turn out to be their strengths. I wouldn't be surprised if that is true of you, Mercy. You seem like a woman who deliberately hides the strongest part of herself."

Mercy's lips parted in surprise. It wasn't just what he said, but the way he said it, the way he looked at her as if he saw the strength he was describing was tangible as her arm or her hair. As if he looked into her soul and really saw her.

They had unconsciously scooted closer to each other during the conversation. The noise of the crowd, the excessively loud band, the clanging of metal by the crew that was setting up the fireworks in the staging area, none of that intruded on their own little bubble. He lowered his face to hers and kissed her. She brushed his tongue with hers and allowed him to explore her mouth. Heat rushed to her body, bringing sweet tingles to her sensitive places. A deep yearning for more filled her. Part of it was pure desire. She wanted to rip the buttons off his shirt and straddle him while she licked his muscular chest like candy. But it was more than lust. She had gone on dates with handsome men before and she had never felt this level of connection.

Their conversation had become so intimate that she had to remind herself he didn't actually know any of her deep dark secrets. Nor was she able to tell him. He looked at her *as if* he could really see her, but there was no way he could. He was human, mundane. If he saw her in her

Valkyrie form, he would probably just laugh, because to him it would look like cosplay.

If only I could be myself with someone like him. She sighed. She broke off the kiss and hid her turmoil by tucking her head against his chest. He stroked her hair. It felt wonderful, which only made her feel miserable. *Why I did accept a date with a human when I knew this would be impossible to take any further? The closer we grow the worse the heartache when we have to break it off.*

As if to emphasize just how abnormal her life was, a ghost had been trying to get her attention the entire time she was talking to Miles. Ghosts had no respect for holidays. The ghost had appeared at the periphery of her vision but drifted closer and closer. First, the ghost had hovered on the far side of the field. Then it reappeared closer to their blanket, hovering over a family that was unpacking fried chicken for dinner. Then the ghost was only one blanket over, sitting in a lawn chair. Mercy realized it was going to reach their blanket, and she knew she would not be able to concentrate on her conversation with Miles while listening to the ghost at the same time. She would embarrass herself.

The band switched from playing popular music to patriotic songs. Mercy said, "I think that's the sign that they're going to start the fireworks soon. And we haven't gotten dinner yet."

"I was waiting for the concession stand lines to go down, but they seem to have only gotten longer," he apologized.

They had already discussed what they wanted to eat, so Mercy said, "Since the slushies and the hotdogs are in two different concession stands, how about I go get the hotdogs and you stand in line for the slushies? That way we won't have to spend time in two lines because otherwise I don't think we will finish before the show starts."

"How about our blanket? Don't we need to leave someone here to guard it?"

Mercy was appalled. "A blanket thrown down in the field for a fireworks display is a sacred thing. No one will touch it."

Twelve

July 4, Monday Night

MERCY PASSED the ghost as she went to the hotdog stand. She knew it would follow her and it did. It was an older ghost, a faint white blob that had no particular shape. It wasn't the bright pinpoint of light of a pure spirit, but simply a splotch of a spirit that had gotten so lazy it no longer maintained its human form. However, in response to Mercy's attention, the ghost straightened itself up and managed to shake out a clearer outline of a man's body. He was wearing a suit with a collar and lapels that suggested he had passed away sometime in the 1970s.

Mercy took out her cell phone and put it to her ear. It was a trick she had heard about to talk with ghosts in such a way that the people around you didn't think you were talking to yourself. If ghosts harassing her was going to be a thing now, this was something she would have to do more frequently.

"Why are you following me?" she asked. "What's your name and how did you die?"

The woman in line in front of her turned around with a startled expression on her face. The woman flushed and quickly turned to face the front again, but not before Mercy felt her cheeks heat up with embarrassment. Okay, Mercy's brilliant plan needed work. She would have to remember not to blurt out things like "how did you die?"

"I was coming out of the laundromat when I was hit by this truck," whimpered the ghost. "The driver wasn't looking where he was going at all and…"

The ghost indignantly recounted the tale of its woeful death. This was another sign it was an older ghost. Fresh ghosts often could not remember exactly how they died. It probably also meant that this ghost was never meant to become a ghost. It should've passed on. There were plenty of reapers who specialized in the victims of traffic accidents. Too bad this ghost was not one she could recommend to her new reaper friend, Sumiko the Shinigami.

"I'm sorry I can't help you," said Mercy. "I would like to. Believe me. But I can't open the door for you. Look, I'll tell you what. I'm going to a… Special… Convention next week. I will look around for any…um… People like me who can deal with your case."

"Sweetheart," hissed the ghost, "I can't wait for a conference. I need you to do this favor for me, here, now. Can you do that? I think you can. Come on baby, work with me."

The ghost put his arm around her shoulder. Although it wasn't physically real, the spiritual contact caused her skin to trickle into goose-bumps. Mercy delicately flicked the ghost arm off of her and stepped to the side.

Okay, she didn't want to get mean, but this was ridiculous. She glared at the ghost.

"If you are in such a rush, let me call my friend the Shinigami, and she will definitely help get you settled."

The ghost turned a whiter shade of pale. "No, no that won't be necessary…"

~

On his way to the slushie line, Miles past a familiar face. It was John, his friend who worked in construction, who sometimes worked out with him on the nature trail exercise path.

"Hey, how's it going, Miles," John called out.

"Hey, John."

John passed on and the exchange of greetings would've been an insignificant event. Just two guys who vaguely knew each other saying hi at an event they both attended. John didn't stop to talk, and Miles didn't try to stop him. But what struck Miles was that John was one of those who had two of his line of "lights" brightly illuminated, the red and the yellow.

Miles had already figured out that the people with the "lights" turned on were special, and those with two or more lights turned on, were even more unusual. They weren't people he would have guessed, either. Mercy was just a cute nurse who rode a bike to work. John was just a tough but sweet guy who enjoyed a beer after a hard day's work. What made them glow?

It was a mistake to invite Mercy on a date, Miles thought. First of all, he shouldn't have done anything that even came close to what the Magician wanted from him. But Miles had been certain nothing weird would happen. He thought if the Magician tried any tricks, Miles would be able to see through them easily enough. In fact, Miles had figured he needed to provoke the Magician to expose more of his techniques for Miles to discover them.

Was the Magician the one responsible for the strange lights he was seeing? Was there some projection system? Drones with a spotlight? Some hidden apparatus? Or maybe the Magician had done something to Miles himself. Put strange droplets in his eyes or drugged his coffee.

It struck Miles as plausible. But... he didn't believe his own rationalizations anymore. Something had flipped upside down inside him, and now, he realized that he was seeing this phenomenon with his own eyes. It was real, whatever it was.

He wondered if he should've given a little more attention to the scientist guy who claimed there were different forms of physics. Because if this was a con, he couldn't see through it. It was one of the best scams he had ever heard about, but he couldn't understand why a man like Alexander Guiscard would waste time to fabricate an elaborate set up on a nobody like him. Didn't make sense.

Okay, he told himself. *Your old way of looking at the world doesn't add up anymore. Look at it from a different perspective. What if this form of sight is real, just as real as ordinary vision?* When Miles had first started doing yoga, some of his fellow practitioners had tried to interest him in what they called, "the spiritual side of yoga." He vaguely recalled something about glowing, colored circles aligned along a person's spine... There was some exotic word for it, but he couldn't remember.

There were still a few inconsistencies with this perspective, however. The Magician had mentioned nine forms of magic, but Miles only saw seven lights. Miles also couldn't understand why he would have this ability. Was it because he did yoga? Hundreds of thousands of people did yoga. Okay, some of them did claim to be able to see these funny named circles in people, but those were usually spiritual practitioners. As for Miles, he had never had the slightest interest in yoga outside of the exercise. For him it was purely about health and balance, keeping strong and keeping limber.

He felt bad for dragging Mercy into all of this. He searched her out in the line in front of the hotdog stand. Some loser who looked like a refugee from Saturday Night Fever was hitting on her. The scumbag even tried to put his arm around her. Miles wondered if he should go to her rescue, but she sidestepped him and seemed to be handling herself. Probably she wouldn't appreciate a caveman display. So Miles stayed in his lane, but he kept an eye on the jerk bothering her. If he took it too far, Miles would have a word with him.

Miles was so focused on Mercy that he didn't notice someone else come up to him until she squealed in his ear.

"Detective Malone!"

He turned around and saw Gini Brown.

"I'm so happy you're on the case," gushed Gini Brown. "I noticed you were here with *her*, and I figured there could only be one reason."

Miles stepped forward a step as the line moved. Gini wasn't in the line, but she moved with him.

"What do you mean?"

"Her." Gini pointed to Mercy. "That's the nurse from the Veteran's Hospital. I saw her a couple of times when I went to visit there. She's the spooky one I told you about! That's why you're investigating her, right? Undercover. That's why I waited until you were alone to come say hi. Don't worry, I'll go soon. I just wanted to let you know that I am really glad to see you're taking this seriously and looking at the nurse. The one they called the angel of death."

"Who calls her that?" demanded Miles, but Gini looked over his shoulder and said, "She's coming this way, I better go before she sees me."

Gini hurried away. Sure enough, the hotdog line had been faster than the slushie line, and Mercy was coming over to bring him his dog. She waited for him as he finally reached the front of his line and got a blueberry and a raspberry slushie.

Lights in the park flickered. A cheer went out from the crowd. By now, the sun had set, and the sky over the Rockies darkened to deep black, sparkling with stars.

"Oh, I think we better hurry to our blanket. The fireworks are going to start soon," said Mercy.

The man who had been bothering her in the hotdog line hurried to her side. He tried to put his arm around her again. Mercy's smile became quite fixed. She deliberately did not look in the direction of the jerk trying to harass her, but Miles noticed how adroitly she stepped out of the way of his arm.

"Hey, asshole," said Miles. "Leave the lady alone. She already has a date."

The man and Mercy both stared at Miles in shock.

"You can see me?" the jerk asked with a comical degree of astonishment.

As if he wasn't standing right in front of Miles.

"You can see him?" echoed Mercy. She sounded just as shocked.

Now this was just getting weird.

"How can you see me?" asked the jerk. "You're just an ordinary human. I don't see anything special about you. Not like Mercy here. She is my angel..." The jerk once again tried to put his arm around Mercy.

Miles had had enough. He transferred both slushies to one hand.

Then he punched the jerk across the jaw.

Or rather, that is what Miles tried to do. His first went right through the man like he was completely insubstantial. Miles lost his balance and dropped both slushies.

~

Mercy realized two things when Miles tried to punch the ghost. One: he could see ghosts. Two: he had no idea he was seeing a ghost and not a living person. That meant this was probably the first time in his life he had seen a ghost.

And here she thought *she* had it bad. She had never been harassed by ghost before. But at least she knew they existed. She had always been able to see them, they just never approached her and asked things of her.

"Dammit, I dropped the slushies!" cussed Miles.

Mercy started to giggle. "You just saw your first ghost, and you're worried about the slushies?"

He looked at her and then at the ghost next to her. The ghost was having fun with this. He put on a terrible face, pulled his ribcage inside out, thrust his tongue out of his eye socket, and screamed GAAAAAH!

Miles glared at the ghost, neither frightened nor even impressed. He said to Mercy in disgust, "Those two slushies cost me $12 bucks for a little flavored ice and now that's gone. But we need to get back to the blanket or will miss the fireworks."

Mercy was surprised by his calm response, but she nodded in agreement. "Oh, okay."

They went back to the blanket, and they did not speak of what had happened. With all the noise and exploding razzle-dazzle in the sky, it would have been hard to have a serious conversation. Then they had to fight the crowds to get out of the park and head home. By then Mercy was tired and not sure what was going on with Miles. He had absolutely seen the ghost. But that didn't necessarily mean he was arcane instead of mundane. Mundanes who were sensitive did occasionally see ghosts; it was one reason that the belief in them was more widespread than belief in other arcanes among ordinary humans.

But his reaction had been strange. The ghost had not frightened Miles, but his apparent dismissal of the whole event suggested he was rejecting magic, like any normal mundane would do. On the other hand, as she herself could testify, it was also a trick that arcanes would pull when they didn't want to admit what they were, even to other arcanes.

She enjoyed the rest of the evening, but the closeness she had felt with him before was gone. It was ironic that they had discussed the importance of trust and sharing what was going on in one's life as the basis of a relationship, but when it came down to it, neither of them was willing to do it.

Thirteen

July 5, Tuesday

MILES DIDN'T GO on his morning jog on Tuesday. He wasn't sure how he'd feel if he saw John.

The court order had worked like magic—as promised—and Miles had a huge stack of papers to go through, as well as access to online files. Nothing on the surface seemed wrong. Yes, the hospital suffered unexpected losses, but also saved many lives that had been assumed to be beyond hope. Dr Cornel was associated with many of those. Apparently, he was a great doctor.

Miles looked for other patterns of malfeasance too, things that might motivate a murder, like pilfered drugs. The Veteran's Hospital, however, seemed to have the opposite "problem." Drugs were ordered for a long regimen, but the patient "recovered fully," and didn't need to take all the doses. The extra doses didn't disappear, at least not according to the records. He'd have to check if the real supplies matched up.

Miles Malone spent a few hours looking through the files before his eyes blurred and his head ached. It had been a mistake to skip his run and yoga that morning, he decided. Sometimes a man needed to hang upside down to see things clearly.

He decided to go for a walk, but not in the woods. Instead, he headed to Main Street, where he encountered a reasonable amount of pedestrian traffic, summer tourists and locals, streaming along the sidewalk, hobnobbing with each other, visiting shops, eating ice cream, having fun. Normal stuff. Miles watched them.

He'd always enjoyed People Watching. Now he did it with new intensity. Now he looked for their inner lights.

Everyone had the lights, but the majority of the tourists had lights that were "closed," and dim, rather than "open," and shining. A few of them displayed one or two lights that were shining and open. Now that he knew what to look for, he could see more complexity in the patterns. The lights weren't simply spheres, but complex three-dimensional polygons, each center a different shape. When they shone most brightly, they also moved, like gears shifting around inside.

Among the locals, the ratio was reversed. More than half of them had at least one shining, open light; a few had two or more illuminated.

All seven lights open—he didn't see any of those in the first two hours that he walked back and forth along Main Street and the other little streets of downtown Arcana Glen.

And then he found one.

A woman walked by him who was lit up like a Christmas Tree. Shocked, Miles concealed his excitement, and, discretely, shadowed her. Physically, she was non-descript. He wouldn't have guessed she was a sorceress of great power, or whatever it was she was that meant she had seven shining lights.

She turned into a sporting goods store that specialized in hiking boots and other outdoor footwear. The store wasn't large, so Miles waited a few minutes before he went in, so it wouldn't be obvious he was following her. He watched the door the whole time, so he was certain she didn't leave again.

Inside the shoe store, there were only two rows to hide in. Miles strolled along both. The check-out counter was crewed by a young man. The only other customer was man with a graybeard who purchased the shoes he had tried on and left.

Miles looked for a back door, but this store didn't have one, only an employees-only bathroom. Miles peered inside. Toilet, sink, mop in a bucket. Empty.

"I'm sorry sir, that bathroom is for employees only," the guy at the checkout counter said.

"Excuse me," said Miles, "Did you see a woman come in here a few minutes ago?"

"Uh..."

"She's my wife," Miles lied with a bright smile. "She told me to meet her at the shoe store, but I wasn't sure which one."

"Uh... a woman came in here but..." The employee noticed there was no one else in the store. "I guess she left."

"Thanks," said Miles.

Magic. It had to be magic. He couldn't get the thought out of his head. Maybe the Magician could have set up some elaborate special effects prank for the Fourth of July, but what explained the inner lights that Miles could still see today? Or a woman who could vanish into thin air?

A lot of things, a stubborn voice inside him insisted. *A man who performs tricks for a living planted an idea in your head. Don't fall for it.*

July 6, Wednesday

The fact that Gini Brown had called Mercy the angel of death bothered Miles so much that he realized he wasn't going to be able to let it rest. He decided to return to the Veteran's Hospital specifically to ask about her this time. Like it or not, she had become a suspect in his case.

He also had to wonder if she was yet another person in this town who knew the Magician. What was that nonsense about seeing ghosts? The guy had been right there. Yet when Miles tried to punch him, it was like punching a hologram. Yeah, a hologram. That's probably how they did it! But it bothered him to think Mercy was in on that deception.

Do you still really think all of this is just a trick? an inner voice mocked Miles. He pushed the thought away.

This time the first person at the hospital that Miles spoke with was Dr. Cornel. Dr. Cornel did not have any circles in his traffic light turned on. He was just a normal guy. If he really was the miracle worker that so many of the people Miles had talked to said he was, it didn't show in the inner light of Dr. Cornel's core.

"Tell me about the RN you sometimes work with, Mercy Wise," Miles urged Cornel. "I've heard she has an interesting nickname."

"Nickname? I'm not aware of any nickname."

"That's interesting, because I heard she was called the angel of mercy. You know, kind of a play on her name."

"Now that you mention it," said Dr Cornel, "I believe I've heard her called the angel of death by some of the patients."

"So she does have a nickname?"

Dr. Cornel hesitated. "If you like. I wouldn't have called it a nickname. More like... A superstition. It's just a coincidence of course, but the patients have noticed that several of the men who have died unexpectedly were either her patients or received visits from her."

"Received visits? Does she visit patients who are not part of her work?"

"Yes, quite frequently. It's unusual, but not against the rules."

"Did she visit Gawain Herle?"

"Quite frequently," said Dr Cornel.

"Dr Cornel, I wonder if you could tell me about a medical breakthrough... I heard of something called a 'jewel'... like if it is used in extreme cases, it can turn them around..."

Cornel's eyes lit up. His chakras, Miles noted, remained dull. Cornel had no magic. So his next words were surprising.

"Do you believe in magic, Mr Malone? How about miracles?"

"I'm coming to," Miles said dryly.

"This is a miracle of science, the magic of technology!" Cornel declared triumphantly. "What I am about to show you is highly classified, so you may not divulge it to anyone. I only share it with you because you have a court order."

Thank you, Alephander Guiscard, Miles said silently. "I'm eager to see this miracle."

Cornel took a small key from his desk and unlocked a cabinet at the back of his office. He opened the door to reveal shelves of evenly spaced crimson jewels on black stands, like smart phones on display in a tech store. Each jewel was the same size, about the size of a golf ball. They sparkled like rubies, but they couldn't be real rubies… the value would be incalculable. Miles, who had amassed a mountain of useless trivia in his eidetic memory, knew that most valuable ruby in the world, the Sunrise Ruby, was a 25.59-carat (5.1 g) Burmese "pigeon blood" ruby, mounted by Cartier and set between heptagonal diamonds. These jewels, if they had been real, would have made the Sunrise Ruby blush.

"Those are medical devices?" Miles asked.

"It works on an entirely new principle of science," declared Cornel. "They infuse regenerative energy into the body at the cellular level. The technology was developed by the military. Thanks to his connections to the base nearby, Dr Winters is able to get a supply to us. Still, we don't have many, and each one can be used only once. Look…" Cornel showed Miles a clear gemstone, which looked like a cheap, plastic toy version of a diamond. "Once drained, the substrate can only be disposed of."

Cornel placed the used gem into a biological disposal container. "I give the used substrates back to Dr Winters to be disposed of at the base, at his request."

"You said Dr Winters procures them from the base. Does he use these jewels too? What about Dr Sharpe?"

"Dr Sharpe is a fool! He confuses technology with magic. He thinks I'm into 'crystal healing' or some absurd New Age nonsense. Dr Winters… he's too proud. He is happy to let me use the jewels, but he thinks if he has to use them, it disparages his own skill. Foolish, in my opinion. I only wish we had more of the jewels, I would use them for every patient! As it is, I must ration them, and use the jewels only on the worse cases."

"What about Miguel Ramos? Gawain Herle?" asked Miles. "Might these miracle jewels have worked on them?"

"Yes—I am sure of it!" declared Cornel. "If only we had known about the condition ahead of time! Alas, even doctors are only human."

～

Miles next tracked down Dr Winters. Dr Winters had not agreed to see him. And when Miles arrived, there was another man in his office speaking with him. Miles only saw the other man from behind.

With his new sight, Miles saw something astonishing. First, Dr Winters had one of the lights in this traffic stack illuminated, the yellow one. But what was more astonishing was the man with Winters. All seven lights were extremely radiant, so strong, in fact, that Miles, for the first time had a hard time seeing the actual physical features of the man himself. Two of the lights, the blue and the purple, were composites, like a yin and a yang swirling together. The blue was composed of shadow and brightness, like a cloud in a sky, while the purple seemed to also be composed of two opposites. And the men talking to Dr Winters had all seven lights illuminated—unless he counted the Yin-yang lights as double, in which case it would be *nine* lights.

Is this what I was supposed to be looking for all along? Miles wondered. *Is this what the Magician was talking about? Is this what it looks like to see a man who has all nine forms of magic?*

Dr Winters noticed Miles standing outside his door. Dr Winters got up and closed the door.

Deciding to be rude because it was worth the opportunity to get a closer look at the man with all nine lights, Miles shoved open the door and let himself in. "I'm sorry to bother you both but I really need to..."

Miles looked around. There was no one else in the office. There was no other exit.

"I'm sorry," said Mr Winters, repressively. "But I really don't have time to talk to you right now. Please leave or I will call security."

"Sorry," said Miles. "I actually didn't want to talk to you. I wanted to talk to the guy you were with."

"I have no idea what you're talking about," said Dr Winters. He stood up and moved toward Miles in a manner that was vaguely threatening. One light in his traffic stack started to rotate, like the winding an old-fashioned stopwatch. Miles felt a strange pressure against his body, as if the air inside the office had become so thick and dense that it pushed him out the way. He felt his body lifted up and moved, the way water lifted a toy boat out of an overflowing tub.

And then he was standing outside the threshold of the office.

Winters sneered at him. Winters did not touch the door, and yet the door slammed in Miles' face.

∼

July 6, Wednesday

Mercy sensed someone using Elemental Wind power as she approached Dr. Winter's office. She saw Miles practically blown out of the room and the door slam in his face.

He glanced up at her. His expression was inscrutable.

Mercy wanted to speak to him about their date. They hadn't discussed meeting again. Had he enjoyed himself? Did he like her? She wanted to spend more time with him, but the ghost had ruined everything. Now she felt more awkward around him than ever.

Rather than bring up anything personal, she tried to imagine why he had been trying to enter Dr Winter's office.

"Are you still investigating the death of Gawain Herle?" she asked.

Miles nodded. He seemed wary, as he had ever since the ghost incident at the park. Mercy's heart sank. This was another promising guy that was going to reject her because of her nature and her involvement in worlds beyond those he could see. Maybe her parents were right. If she just did Valkyrie work in Valhalla, she would only meet men who already knew about her dual nature and not only didn't mind it but respected it. But what was there for a Valkyrie to do in Valhalla besides paperwork? The whole point of being a Valkyrie was to guide those who needed passage to Dayhaven, not to sit around filling out forms.

Although, the humans on earth also managed to make her spend a lot of time filling out forms. She held a whole stack of them in her arms right now as a matter of fact.

"Was Dr Winters helpful?" she asked.

"Extremely," said Miles sarcastically.

They stared at each other awkwardly for another long moment. Mercy hoped he would ask her out on a second date. Why not do it herself? After all, it wasn't that she held any old-fashioned ideas about making the males do all the asking. But she found herself too nervous to be rejected. How did guys do it anyway?

"I had fun at the fireworks," she said.

"Me too." His smile seemed genuine, but he didn't take the hint and ask her out a second time.

She sighed and gave up on the idea of any future between them. Whatever they had, whatever spark she imagined, it had already died.

"Well," she said, "Pardon me, but I have to speak to Dr Winters."

Miles decided to shamelessly eavesdrop on Mercy's conversation with Dr Winters. At first it did not seem to be anything important. She had paperwork and she needed his signature on some of it. But just when Miles was about to move away from the door so he wouldn't be caught in an embarrassing position, he heard her clear her throat as if she were uncomfortable. Miles instinctively paused to hear what made her so nervous.

Miles heard Mercy ask Dr Winters, "I noticed that you have been asking for quite a few of the patients to be transferred. I have to wonder why. The military base where you want them to go is not a hospital, and it is definitely not a Veteran's Hospital."

"Since the military base is top secret, and even its existence should not be known to you, I don't see how you could know what facilities they have or do not there, Nurse Wise," Dr Winters replied coldly.

"I would just like to know what reason you have to transfer these patients. Most of these are doing well here, and some of them you even requested to transfer when they were supposed to be entirely released from here. I don't understand the logic behind it. Perhaps if you could explain..."

"I do not need to explain myself to you. I know what you are and what you are really doing here, Miss Wise. I suggest if you do not want me to tell anyone else, that you learn to mind your own business as well."

There was a long silence and then Miles heard her move toward the door. He hurried away before she could see him waiting in the hall.

Fourteen

July 6, Wednesday

MILES DUCKED BEHIND A CORNER. He waited for Mercy to leave the office and then at a suitable distance he started trailing her. Shadowing someone inside a hospital was much more difficult than shadowing them on the street. But he was able to follow her to the floor with the long-term patients, those whose prognosis was not favorable.

She was visiting the patients, just as Dr. Cornel had described. It wasn't clear to Miles if she had any business doing so. She checked their charts and their IV drips and the little screens next to their beds. If they needed to have a bed pan changed or requested a cup of water, she provided it. As far as he could tell she was just being a good nurse. She was, in fact, the kind of nurse every sick man hoped to get but so seldom did: beautiful, cheerful, ready to help and able to anticipate her patient's needs.

One of the patients was different than the others. There was a certain rattle in his throat that even Miles could tell did not sound good. But Mercy's response was astounding. She did not summon one of the doctors. She did not call for other nurses or for an EMP or for more medicine.

"

Instead, she stepped away from the bed. She spread out her arms, and she spun around like Wonder Woman and transformed into an amazon with a winged helmet and huge metal wings. She was wearing a chain mail bikini like Red Sonja. She then bent back over the bed, patted the patient's chest...

...and then reached *into his chest with her hand.*

No blood spurted. The patient did not respond physically. It was like when Miles punched his fist through the man at the Fourth of July celebration. But in this case, Mercy pulled the ghost *out of the body.* Miles could see the exact duplicate of the man's physical body as an eerie glowing white outline. Then, even as Miles watched, the old wrinkly ghost shed his years and became a strapping young soldier in his uniform. Mercy let go of his ghostly hand and saluted him. He saluted back.

Out of nowhere, a wooden Door with a brass handle appeared in the room.

Mercy opened the magic Door that had not even been there a moment before. Together the two of them stepped across the threshold.

The door disappeared and so did Mercy and the soul of the soldier.

Mercy was surprised to see that Miles was still outside the hospital at the end of her shift. She knew that he had stopped asking questions inside the hospital hours ago. Had he been waiting here all that time or he had gone somewhere else and come back?

Of course, she had also gone somewhere else and come back, but she had escorted a Warrior's soul to Valhalla, so that was hardly the same.

"Can I talk to you?" Miles asked.

"Is this about the case you are investigating?" she parried.

"Actually, it's about another case." He paused, then added, watching her carefully, "One the magician asked me to investigate."

"The Magician! You don't...?!" She lowered her voice and leaned toward him. "Surely you don't mean you're investigating the Massacre of the Guardians?"

"You know about it."

"Every arcane knows about it."

"What's an arcane?" asked Miles.

She looked bewildered. "How do you know about the Massacre, but you don't know something like that?" But then Mercy remembered the ghost. "This is all new to you, isn't it? Were you raised by humans?"

"I used to think so," said Miles dryly. "Now I'm not so sure of anything. Are you trying to ask if I'm human? I don't have pointy ears, so I guess I'm not an Elf. And I don't turn into... Whatever the hell it is you are when you put on your chain mail bikini and opera helmet."

Mercy pressed her lips together. "I'll walk my bicycle home and we can talk on the way."

"Okay."

"So..." Where to begin. Mercy glanced sidelong at Miles. He seemed calm. If this was truly new to him, shouldn't he be freaking out?

She had heard of situations like this but had never encountered it before. There were arcanes who were raised in the human world and never knew what they were until their power started to manifest. Or, it could be that he had been born an ordinary mundane, but encountered an event that had transformed him. Sometimes ordinary humans were Called by the Light to receive powers. The Light could Call anyone. No one knew why.

Mercy decided to start with the basics.

"Arcanes are people with magic. Usually, arcanes are also people who are not from earth. I don't mean aliens, I mean from a difference Sphere."

"Is that why you wouldn't tell me what foreign country you grow up in? It wasn't even this Sphere?"

"That's right. I am a Valkyrie. You may have heard of us..."

"You're a Valkyrie," he repeated flatly. His brow furrowed. At least he wasn't laughing. "And you work in a Veteran's Hospital... I think I understand now. Does that mean you're the one killing these men? Do you think you're taking them to Valhalla?"

"I'm not killing anyone! My job is not to kill. My job is to escort souls of those who have already died to their next destination. "

"So that's why they call you the angel of death."

"Technically, I *am* a type of reaper. Reapers can be either Daemons or Angels... Angels are what you call those of us who live in Dayhaven, although in other traditions we were referred to as demigods or lesser gods."

"You're saying you're actually a goddess?"

"No, I'm saying that I am actually just a person like you. We are born, we grow up, we get married, we have children, and we die. Dayhaven is what many of your people consider to be heaven, but it is not what we consider to be the Last Home, where souls return to the full presence of the Light. But it is the destination of many souls after they have spent time on earth, before they are ready to move on to the Last Home."

Mercy waited quietly for a while, but Miles didn't speak. Finally, unable to bear the silence, she asked, "Do you understand? Do you have other questions?"

"I'm thinking about all this," he admitted. "It's a lot to take in. What about the lights?"

"What lights?

"The lights that you have in you. The colored lights that make a line... I'm not describing it well, I'm sorry. I can't remember the terminology."

Now it was Mercy's turn to furrow her brow. "Is this something that you see when you look at people?"

"It just started recently. Actually, just yesterday when we went to the Fourth of July celebration together." He tried once again to explain what he saw, but it only confused Mercy further.

"How strange..." she mused. "It's a very unique power, nothing I've heard of specifically... But seeing visions in people's auras is something I do understand. I have a similar power. When I see people, I see how much lifeforce they have remaining. If it's low, then I know they are near death. It doesn't necessarily mean they'll die, but it is a sign that they might. To me it looks like an Hourglass."

"Do you see that for everyone?"

"Everyone who is supposed to be here. Ghost don't have it, because they are no longer supposed to be in this Sphere."

"Can you see mine?"

"Yours is very strange."

"What? What's so strange about it?"

"It spins. The first time I saw it, it looked sideways to me, like an infinity sign, but later, right now, for instance, I could see that it is actually slowly spinning. It means that you're alive but you're not advancing toward death. I can't quite explain it. I've never seen anything like that, not even in very powerful beings. Even Elves and Dragons who have very long lives still have a normal Hourglass. But not you."

Miles frowned so deeply that Mercy felt terrible. "I'm sorry, you've already had so much to deal with just finding out that the arcane world is real and now I've added this as well."

"I'd rather have all the evidence I can gather. Whether it's disturbing or not. I just have to figure out how everything fits together."

"What do you see when you look at me?" she asked curiously. "Do you see that column of lights?"

"Yes. One seems to come from here..." He gently stroked her throat. "And the other seems to float just above here." He touched the top of her head, where her bangs met the part in her hair. His fingers on her hair sent delicious shivers down her spine.

She went very still, suddenly aware of him as a physical being and herself as a woman responding to his touch.

"After the way the Fourth of July ended, I thought you might not want to see me again," she confessed.

Miles jerked his hand away from her face. "Listen, Mercy... I don't want to lead you on... I have a lot on my plate right now..."

Mercy suppressed the little scream of disappointment that echoed against the locked walls of her hollow heart. She smothered her disappointment with a big smile.

"You are just discovering that legends you've dismissed as fantasy are real. And I can't believe it, but apparently the Magician has hired you to investigate the Massacre of the Guardians."

"You don't have to sound so surprised." His lips twisted in a wry smile.

"It is surprising, though. That's not any insult, Miles. But I don't think you realize how unusual it is. He doesn't just bring in anybody. He's the most powerful wizard in our world, in any of our worlds. It's... That he would hire a human detective, it's just... It's mind blowing.

And it shows that you probably have some power that he's already recognized that you haven't. It must be related to the lights you see. That is the key to your form of magic. You should find out what that means."

"Do you think I have a magic? I'm no wizard."

"You're definitely unusual. I've never met anybody with a spinning Hourglass before. And you see lights in people's auras. Do you... Do you have any other unusual abilities?"

Miles pressed his lips together and did not answer.

Was there something else he knew about that he didn't want to share with her?

"Where can I learn more about these colored circles that I see glowing from people?" he asked.

Fifteen

"IT'S NOT A DATE," said Mercy. "I understand that you probably don't want to start a new relationship right when you're dealing with all of this. But you asked me about where you could learn more, and this is the perfect place.

"Okay, you can open your eyes now."

They had agreed to meet for a non-date on Main Street. Mercy had ridden her bike and Miles had driven his car and parked a few blocks away. She had made him close his eyes while she dragged him down the sidewalk to whatever surprise she had waiting.

He opened his eyes. "Oh. Yeah, I've passed this store dozens of times. I never even thought about going inside. I drink coffee."

The pretty little shop was called *Tea & Tarot*. Generally, Miles tried to avoid shops that had overly cute names and catered to mystical pretensions. This shop did both.

"The shop owner is a very nice Elf named Bella," said Mercy, "Although, lately, her daughter Tia or another young woman is usually the one working. There's even a shop girl who works here who is like you in some ways. She was born completely human but called to magic as an adult. I'm not sure exactly what her power is, only that her Hourglass changed after she developed magic. Her lifespan dramatically increased. So, there's that advantage of becoming an arcane. Although, in your case I don't know how that would apply, since I can't even tell if you have a lifespan in the usual sense of the term."

As they entered the shop, a bell over the door rang. A cheerful young woman in her twenties called to them from the counter. "Good morning! I'm Tia. Let me know if I can help you find anything."

Miles shrugged and went over to the counter. "Actually, yes. I am looking for books on a kind of magic ball."

"Magic ball?" Tia crinkled her nose in puzzlement.

The shop girl looked at Mercy, but Mercy only shrugged. "It's not my field. From what he described to me; it sounds like some kind of alchemical thing. Symbols used by mages."

"Oh." From Tia's expression, it was clear this did not narrow things down.

"Spinning balls of light with different designs on them, geometrical shapes, maybe numbers, in a row down the spine, starting with white and going in rainbow order to red." Miles demonstrated on his own torso, drawing an imaginary line from just above his head down to his jeans.

"Do you mean chakras?" asked Tia. "By the Light, we have a whole section on that!"

Miles followed her to a portion of the bookstore where he saw book after book with illustrations that were obviously trying to capture the same images he had seen. The cartoon images were not quite as three-dimensional as the real-life version, of course. They didn't quite capture the amazing way the lights seem to pour out from within a person's soul, shining through their body like a light through a piece of paper. But he got the idea, and he knew this was exactly what he had seen. Obviously, he wasn't the only person throughout history who had factually perceived this.

Up until till now he would've dismissed all this as mumbo-jumbo, but try as he might to imagine how the Magician might have somehow used technology to project the lights on to people, Miles could no longer believe that explanation. For instance, right now, when he looked at Tia, he could see that she had the usual seven centers down the core of her body, but only one of them was faintly illuminated. If she had magic, perhaps it was weak?

"This is it," he said. "Thank you, I can take it from here."

"Just let me know ...I'll be right over there."

He knelt down so that he could look at some of the big books on the lower shelves. He found books on yoga as well, including some that seem to be practical manuals. Maybe he had made a mistake not to come to the store before, even from the point of just improving his form during his physical exercise. He added one to the pile of other books he was stocking up.

"My goodness, are you going to buy all of those?" asked Mercy.

"You are the one who told me I should find out what I am. I don't understand any of this but apparently this is part of my world now. I need to master it if I'm going to help on the case the Magician gave me. I'm sorry if it's boring for you, you don't have to stay..."

"Not at all. I was just thinking I should come in here more often. I'm going to browse. Take your time and don't worry about me."

She moved to another part of the store and Miles continued his search. Some of the manuals seemed very basic. And many of them seem to have the same sort of information. He didn't want to buy every single one... There are too many for him to afford and read, but he wanted to get a good selection. He flipped through them carefully, perusing the contents and making evaluations with an eye to finding information not related to his actual visions.

Another customer entered the store. It was another young woman who seemed to know Mercy already. He heard them chatting in another aisle. He relaxed a little, no longer feeling as guilty for wasting Mercy's time while he shopped for books.

In fact, she was still talking by the time he had found what he needed for now. He took his pile and continued to walk down different aisles of the bookstore, looking out for anything that might be helpful. He came to a series of books on Runes and Norse mythology. When he found a book on Valkyries, he surreptitiously added this to his pile.

～

Sumiko Sadukatzu, the Shinigami, entered the shop. She and Mercy fell into talking shop. Mercy smiled. It was so nice to have another reaper friend.

"I am so excited for the conference," said Mercy.

"Me too!" The other woman said. "I have heard a rumor that they are going to announce open auditions for the new Guardian of Death. Do you think that's possible?"

"Is that a kind of thing they have auditions for?" Mercy asked. "Isn't it just whoever is the strongest reaper?"

"Yes, but how would they determine that?"

"I don't know... It's not like reaping souls is a competitive sport."

"Speak for yourself," laughed the other girl. "Our people often keep score of who has the biggest number of hits on the hunt for evil ghosts. My score is quite high. Not high enough that I think I have a chance at becoming the new Guardian of Death though."

"Would you even want to? It would be like getting an office job after fieldwork, wouldn't it?" Mercy shrugged. "What does the Guardian of Death do anyway? They don't reap souls directly. They just... what? Oversee other reapers? Sounds tedious."

"How are you going to compete for the position if you don't even know what the Guardian does?" teased Sumiko. "Yes, they make sure that there are reapers assigned to all the souls that need to be reaped. New categories come up all the time. There couldn't be a reaper who collected souls from car accidents before there were cars. The number of reapers used to collect the souls of those who died of smallpox has gone down, but the number of souls to collect from those who died of cancer has gone up. And when there are too many reapers in a field, the Guardian has to prevent them from fighting each other.

"Finally, if there are Rogue Souls that no reaper is able to collect, the Guardian does do some fieldwork to collect those. I have even heard of a Rogue Soul right here in Arcana Glen who refused to die. If the Guardian of Death doesn't stop it, then this greedy soul will disrupt the whole balance of nature."

Mercy had heard rumors about Rogue Souls. When a reaper came to get a dying soul, sometimes the person thought he would be clever, and kill the reaper, then leap back into his body. Unfortunately, with enough magic, or dumb luck, it sometimes worked, but it always created bad karma. What did a Rogue Soul look like?

Recalling the strange Hourglass of Miles Malone, she peered at him a bit anxiously.

Miles waved at her from the checkout stand. He had a huge bag of books. "Are you getting anything?"

She showed him a healing crystal that she had bought. Some of her patients had strong Elemental Earth magic, and they benefited the most from these crystals. They also appreciated that she recognized their form of magic and helped them acquire charms they were not in a position to get at the hospital.

She squinted a little as if trying to see if his spinning Hourglass was still abnormal. It was still there, and an odd tilt right now, looking very still, unless she stared at it for a long time. She could see it slowly ticking like the hour hand of a clock. In fact, right now it was almost fully upright, and the grains of sand were sliding from the top to the bottom. If he had been an ordinary mortal, she would have guessed he was going to have a deadly encounter in a few days. But she could not guess what was going to happen with someone like Miles.

How ironic that when she met him, she had wished he were anything other than human. But now that she knew he did have some powers, it frightened her even more. If he was a Rogue Soul, illegally trying to escape the bonds of life and death, that would make them enemies.

"Listen, Mercy, there's something I have to confess to you," he said as they left the store. A little bell rang when they open the door. Miles turned and waved goodbye to Tia. "Thank you!"

"Thank you!" she echoed. "Come again sometime!"

Miles continued his thought on the other side of the door back out on the main sidewalk. "I feel bad because I asked you out on a date for the wrong reasons. The truth is—I was told to get a date. That's why I asked if you would go with me to the picnic."

"You... weren't really interested in me?" Mercy asked. She swallowed.

"I wouldn't say I wasn't interested in you. And to prove it, let me take you to dinner. There's a restaurant in town that I've been hearing about ever since I got here. I've never gone because I hate sitting at a table alone in public. And I've never had a woman that I wanted to take there. Until now."

"I don't think that's a good idea." Mercy wouldn't look at him. "I think that probably you and I should not date. I'm glad to help you, because I know it can be overwhelming finding out about all of this. Not that it's happened to me. I grew up knowing about it. But I have friends who found out only when they were closer to your age. My point is, I want to help you, but please don't think that this will lead anywhere. I am... I'm not interested in a romantic relationship."

"With me. You meant to add those words, but you were too polite." Miles grimaced. "I don't think you would've accepted an invitation to go to the Fourth of July picnic if you weren't interested at all in a romantic relationship. But now something has changed, and for some reason you don't want to go out with me."

She stammered and blushed and tried to deny it but only ended up looking like what he said was correct.

"Just tell me this," he said, "Is it me personally?" he asked. "My personality, which I know is somewhat prickly? Or my smell? Do I stink?" He sniffed his armpits. "I stink, don't I? You know, that could be solved with a good deodorant."

She was starting to laugh helplessly. "No, you smell nice."

"Damn, if I smell nice, then it's definitely my personality. Unless it's my looks. It's the ears, isn't it? By the way, what happens to your ears when you're in your other form? It looks like they turn into wings. But I've never heard of a creature with wings on its head before."

"Uh...It's complicated..."

"You could explain it to me over dinner. Not as a date, just as a friend who is helping me understand this new world. Just like today, when we met here at the bookstore. That wasn't too bad, was it?"

"I should say no."

"Why?"

Because, she thought privately, he could tell her and she could tell herself that it wasn't a date, but they both knew if they had dinner together it would feel like a date. And she was already starting to have feelings for him.

What could she say? That she wanted to find out if he was using his magic for evil? But what if he was totally innocent and she was just accusing him based on some rumors shared by her Shinigami friend who had only had her license to reap for a few years?

"My parents want me to marry a reaper," she blurted. "Or one of the Warriors in Valhalla."

"I see. That's right, I forgot that in your homeland, magical Norway, they still arrange marriages, as if we were living in medieval times. You're okay with that?"

"Not really."

"Mercy, I already made reservations at the restaurant. I'm going to show up there and eat alone if I have to. But I would like it very much if you showed up as well. At 20:00...uh, at 8 o'clock, this Saturday—"

"Wait." She touched his arm. "You really don't mind dating a Valkyrie?"

"Is that a trick question?" he asked suspiciously. "Is this like one of those things where women ask, like 'Which shirt do you like?' and if you pick one, they say, 'Gah, so you think the other one makes me look fat?!' Because I'm terrible at those games. Are you going ask me which of your two forms I find sexier? You as a cute curvaceous brunette or you as a tall statuesque, feathery-eared blonde? Because you're gorgeous to me in both forms, Mercy."

She blushed all the way to her ear lobes. "I was going to say, if I'm going to get dressed up to go out to dinner, you better pick me up in your car. Because I'm not going to ride a bicycle in high heels."

Sixteen

July 11, Monday

MILES TRIED an experiment when he met up with his friend John on the jogging path early Monday morning. Clear as day, Miles could see that John had two chakras lit up, but what did that mean?

Why not come out and ask him point blank?

"Did you have a good Fourth?" asked Miles, to warm up the conversation.

John grunted. "Could have been worse. Were you with a woman?"

Miles couldn't help but grin. "Yup. And I'm going to see her again this Saturday."

John returned a genuine smile. "That's great. Man, I wish I could… but, nah, that's not likely to happen."

"Because your people have arranged marriages and all that."

"Yeah, and because my grandfather is an ass. He cut me out of his will, but he still steps in to control my life whenever it suits him." John scowled. "Last month he made me do a 'favor' for him that could have cost me bigtime. I was lucky. I came out of it unscratched. No thanks to him."

"You should tell him to suck it."

John smiled but shook his head. "I wish it were that easy. You don't know my family."

Miles wouldn't get a better straight line.

"Hey, John, I was wondering, what kind of arcane are you?" Miles asked.

John froze.

"Is it rude to ask?" Miles said innocently.

John fixed him with a hard stare. He crossed his arms and jutted out his chin. "Ice Giant."

He said it like a challenge.

Ice blue eyes, buzzed blond hair, stature like an ogre...

"That makes sense." Miles nodded.

"Are you arcane?" John asked, still cautious, as if he expected Miles to attack him or something.

"Not that I know of," said Miles. "But my date is."

"No way. Is that where you found out about this? What is she? If you don't mind my asking—you did ask me first," he added pointedly.

"Valkyrie."

John's jaw dropped. "You're shitting me."

"C'mon, I didn't even know Valkyries were real until she told me."

"A *Valkyrie* is dating *you*..." John shook his head. "This world is upside down."

Miles whistled to himself back at his office. It was turning out to be a much better day than he thought. He wondered if he had time to take his nice suit to the dry cleaners. On the other hand, he also wanted to get to work on the books he had purchased. He finally decided to wear his second-best suit to dinner and crack the books. He hoped that wasn't a bad omen, that he was making the same mistake he made before with his first relationship, putting work above the woman he was interested in. But on the other hand, he began to feel there was a certain urgency to both cases. He had a feeling they might even be connected in some way. But maybe it was only because he now suspected magic users were responsible in both the untimely death of Gawain Herle and the Massacre of the Guardians.

He spread the books out on his desk, pulled out his nice fountain pen and a stack of clean crisp 3 x 5 cards and started to go through the books, taking notes. Along with the information he found in the books, he also made a set of notes about his own observations at the Fourth of July picnic. He put the name of the person at the top of the card and then a description of how their traffic lights had looked. Their chakras. If he remembered people he had seen, but didn't know their names, he put a brief description of where he'd seen them and their physical attributes: "Picnic—male, scrawny, 5'4", goatee, pointy nose, wart on side of throat."

The most important thing he gleaned immediately from the books was that a chakra could be either open or closed. He realized that when he saw the traffic lights turned off, this was the same as looking at a chakra that was closed or blocked. A chakra that was turned on, allowing energy to flow from the Light through the individual, was a chakra that was considered open. The books focused on the purpose of opening the chakras for health and spiritual attainment.

None of them except one mentioned the relevance for magic, a tome entitled, "The Elven Guide to Arcane Chakras," by Lewyllen Gwondar, published by the "Arcana Glen Academy" which was an odd coincidence. He noticed that in the beginning of this book, the introduction read: ***This book is for everyone, but especially for you arcanes who are visiting from other spheres. You know who you are.***

Not surprisingly, this book had the most useful information. This book talked about how every one of the seven chakras had a multifaceted nature. The warmer colored chakras, the so-called lower chakras, although they were just as important as the others, were represented by many-sided geometric shapes to show all the different kinds of Elemental Magic each one could express. The higher chakras, the cooler colors, represented psychic powers. Psychic powers included telepathy, empathy, and charisma, but two of the Chakras had a shadow side that also included powers that sounded ominous to Miles, such as mesmerism, dominance, vampirism.

Please don't tell me vampires and werewolves are real too, he thought.

According to this book, they were.

The book even had helpful diagrams showing him how to recognize werewolves (which the book called Wolf Shifters) and vampires just by looking at their chakras when they were in human form. Werewolves were Animal Shifters and activated the chakra used by all shape shifters. Vampires, according to this book, were humans who transformed after being bitten by a demon during a specific ritual. They were addicted to drinking blood, but their real power was psychic; they fed off the pain, despair, and fear of their victims. The blood was only a conduit for them.

Super creepy, thought Miles.

By comparison, Werewolves were just "ordinary" Shifters, who happened to have the power to change into wolves, an impulse that was usually stronger around the Full Moon. Like many other arcanes, silver was a metal that could be especially imbued with magic power to restrain them. Ordinary silver would not suffice, however. It was like blood for vampires, the conduit of a more ethereal form of energy. The bite of a werewolf could not change any ordinary human into a werewolf. Only a specific ceremony could do that, and that ceremony did involve a bite. "This is usually only done to recruit a human mate into the pack," the book noted laconically.

The purple chakra, the mind chakra, was the one that Miles thought should have been involved in things like telepathy, but that wasn't true, according to this book. The duality of the purple chakra was not related to shadow and light. It did have a dual nature, but it was related to time and reality: the past and the future; memories and dreams. Beings who had this chakra open were exceedingly rare and exceedingly powerful.

Miles examined himself in the mirror to see if he could detect his own chakras. He couldn't; neither by looking down at himself, nor by looking in the mirror, nor even by taking a selfie. Sighing, he abandoned the attempt and returned to the book.

The "highest" chakra, the crown chakra, which shone as a pure white light, was called, "Non-Dual." It was the power of spirit. This included the ability to see ghosts. Temporary activation of this chakra in an ordinary person could allow them to communicate with loved ones who had passed. Most people only activated this chakra under such extreme emotional circumstances, and never were able to do so again.

As Miles expected, the ability to use this chakra and keep it open regularly was extremely rare. It meant that a person had the ability to not only see ghosts, but communicate with them, touch them, and actively open Gates (or Doors) between the Spheres to banish ghosts from earth or invite them here from higher Spheres.

All of this was important to Miles because he remembered Mercy had the Spirit (white) chakra open, along with the lighter half of her psychic (blue) chakra. That fit with what she told him that she was: a Valkyrie, a magical being here on earth to guide the souls of dead warriors to an angelic realm on the other side.

I asked this girl to dinner? Miles buried his head in his hands. What a dunce he was. No wonder she had gently tried to inform him that he didn't have a chance with her. *My parents want me to marry a reaper,* she said. And he made some joke about arranged marriages. But what she was really trying to tell him, he realized now, without hurting his feelings, was that she was completely out of his league.

Miles was deep in compiling notes when his secretary rang up on his office phone to let him know he had two visitors.

"They are both scrumptious," Eva added completely unnecessarily. "If only I were young and single again."

Even over the phone, Miles could hear one of the men reply with an Irish lilt, something charming and flirtatious, although Miles couldn't hear the exact words. He rolled his eyes. He could guess who that was.

Sure enough, Owen McGee sauntered in through the office door. Another much more reserved gentleman followed him.

"We were sent to check on how you're doing and give you some more information!" declared Owen McGee. "This is Maverick Cade. He's the one who's going to give you more information, and I just came along to make sure he showed up. He's a little shy."

"I'm not shy," said Maverick.

"Says the man who lives in an isolated secret fort somewhere in the mountains."

"I'm just busy," insisted Maverick.

"Sure, mate," mocked Owen. "Keep telling yourself that."

The man Owen had called Maverick Cade ignored this. He walked up to the desk and dropped a huge pile of three ring binders, each one 3 inches thick, on Miles's desk. Miles raised his eyebrows and picked up the top binder. He opened it and scanned the first several pages. Then he flipped through it and scanned deeper into the paperwork.

Most of it was incomprehensible gibberish to him, equations that looked like something out of a university level physics book, or even a scientific journal. It was way over his head.

"I told the Magician, I don't have the level of math to understand this," said Miles.

"Some of the books have pictures," Maverick said, in a tone that indicated he thought the need for pictures to understand his equations was like the need of a child for a coloring book. Miles doubted that any pictures in this mess of math was going to help him at all.

"The thing is," said Owen. "If you need any computer help you should go to this guy. He's practically a machine himself." Owen laughed like that with some kind of joke.

Maverick, casting Owen a sidelong glance, did not comment.

Miles examined the men's chakras. This was going to be a thing for him now, Miles realized. Not only making notes of a person's physical appearance, like their height, weight and number of visible warts, but which chakras they had open and which they had closed. The scientist had two open chakras, one blue, the "throat chakra," focused on the light "yang," or light, side of the blue. The other chakra was the "heart chakra," which glowed vibrant green, like summer sunlight filtered through trees. The creative vibrancy that throbbed in the lotus shape of the green chakra was not at all what Miles would have expected from the man who appeared almost robotic in his outward mannerisms.

If he had not had this other form of vision, Miles would have described the man's behavior as high functioning autism. Perhaps it was a good reminder: People possessed inner resources that weren't apparent on the surface.

As for Owen McGee, his chakras surprised Miles too. Honestly, after Miles' experiences with Owen's less than firm dedication to legalities, Miles expected to see some dark powers swirling around in Owen's chakras. But his "throat chakra" was activated with Yang, or light magic, as was his "solar plexus chakra," which glowed a happy, golden color.

Without using his chakra vision, Miles would have described Owen McGee as the opposite of the autist in many ways; flexible where the other man was inflexible, comfortable with people, someone who liked to go with the flow and improvise on the spot, someone who was able to wheel and deal. Someone who liked to gamble and suffered huge ups and downs in life because of it, but who always knew how to roll with the punches and come back up on top.

These were his first impressions, but how accurate were they? Miles decided he wanted to spend more time with the two men to test his evaluations, both magical and personal. He needed to get a perspective on this new power he had and the only way he knew to do that was to spend time with people, get to know them, figure them out. He also wanted to see them in a different situation than their work relationship. People acted differently when they were off the clock.

He stretched his arms, not having to feign his kinked sore back and neck.

"Look," said Miles, "I have been working for twelve hours straight now. I was about to kick back with a game on my GamePlayer. I have a pretty sweet set up and plenty of room for guests, do you two want to join me? Your choice of games. We've got first person shooters, online role-plays, racing games..."

"I've heard of these 'video' games," said Owen, sounding intrigued, "But I've never actually had time to play. Is there money involved?"

"There's reputation involved," said Miles. He had no intention of gambling against Owen McGee. He didn't have that many shirts that he could afford to lose them. "I'm an expert, and you're obviously a noob. Let's see if you can take me on."

"What is this game of which he speaks?" asked Maverick.

"What?!" demanded Owen. "Maverick, you're supposed to be good at computers and you've never played a video game?"

"I am very busy," Maverick repeated.

"Or maybe you're just another noob afraid to challenge me on the field of battle," suggested Miles.

"I am not a noob." He looked at Owen. "What is a noob?"

Miles cracked his knuckles and opened the door from his office to his gaming room. "Gentleman, you were about to find out. Prepare to be schooled."

"I don't have time for games," Maverick insisted. "I only came here in person because the Leprechaun demanded it."

"Is that what you are?" Miles smirked at Owen. "Aren't you supposed to have red hair and a green hat?"

"For once," said Owen, "I agree with the robot. We don't have time to play games, human. Too bad, because I bet I could wipe the floor with you, even if it's a game I've never played before."

"Easy words to say when you're about to run away," taunted Miles. He appealed to the Leprechaun on a more serious note. "Play with me, it will help me figure out the case."

"There is no known relationship between playing a game and solving a murder," said Maverik.

"That you've discovered *yet*," corrected Miles. "What I find is that sometimes doing something completely different while trying to think about a case in the back of your mind can help you find a new perspective."

"Okay," said the Leprechaun. "That sounds like bullshit to me too, but you're the one the Magician said to make happy. You're the flavor of the month so we'll try it your way. But we can't stay long. Forty minutes, tops. Pick a game we can finish in that amount of time."

Miles pulled out *Warriors of Wysteria*. "This should be short and sweet."

Five hours later, around three in the morning, Miles had discovered three things. One: the Leprechaun had completely bullshitted him about never playing video games before. In fact, Owen already had the top avatar in Warriors of Wysteria, a Dragonslayer, plus diamond armor, an electrum scythe, and infinite Good Fortune, one of the top charms.

It was a good thing that Miles had refused to bet any money on the game. Otherwise, even with the money the Magician had promised, and that Eleni had paid him, Miles would've found himself in debt to the damn Leprechaun.

Two: Maverick had told the honest truth that he had never in his life played a single video game before.

Three: Maverick really was a robot. A magical robot, but still a robot.

The robot wiped the floor with both of them.

Seventeen

July 13, Wednesday

MERCY TOLD herself that the upcoming date was no big deal. Nonetheless, she went shopping to buy a new dress. She even bought new make up as well at Forever Fairy, a boutique in town.

Every morning when she rode by on her bicycle, Miles waved at her. She started leaving for work earlier and earlier, so she'd have time to exchange a few words with him. No matter how early she passed his balcony, he was already there; on Wednesday, she left forty minutes early, and he invited her up share a bagel and orange juice.

"Tell me about your investigations," she said. "What progress have you made? If you don't mind discussing it with me..."

"I don't mind at all," he said. "It's something I miss from my days of working in the detective's bull pen in Denver. Sometimes talking with another detective would help me test out various lines of inquiry that might lead to breaking a case wide open."

"I'm glad you think of me as a detective now, and not a suspect," she smiled.

"Everyone is always a suspect," said Miles. "As you know, Gini

Brown thinks that there's something strange about her boyfriend's death."

"Gawain Herle, right?"

Miles nodded. "When I first checked Herle's medical records, I was puzzled. His injury was described as a 'broken hind leg,' which I thought was just a typo at the time. The wound was from an IED that exploded when he was entering a suspect dwelling."

"We do get a lot of battlefield wounds," said Mercy. "That's one of the many reasons I work at the Veteran's Hospital."

"Right," said Miles. "But it struck me as odd that he wasn't treated in the Landstuhl Regional Medical Center in Germany. That's where all medivacs from Iraq and Afghanistan would be taken."

Mercy bit her lip. "I assumed it was because he was an arcane that they sent him to Arcana Glen."

"But surely there are arcanes all over the world, aren't there?"

Mercy nodded. "Yes. You're right. There was nothing about his injury that couldn't have been treated by arcane doctors in Germany. For that matter, his injury could be treated by mundane doctors. I just never thought about it."

"It's not something that you would have to worry about," he said. "As I dug deeper, I discovered that Herle's nickname in his squad was Centaur, which at the time struck me as odd. But then I thought that the entry on the medical record was just a practical joke." He paused. "Now, I suspect that it wasn't."

Mercy smiled, her whole face shining with mirth. "No, not really. Gawain Herle really was a Centaur Shifter. Kind of rare, but actually quite an asset in battle."

"I bet they are, because they're always at the *centaur* of the action."

Mercy groaned.

"Do any centaurs work at the hospital?" he asked.

"No..."

"They're probably all at the *Centaur* for Disease Control."

"Will you stop!" She broke into giggles. "Where do you come up with these?"

"I've got a million on these. I have a joke about a Satyr too, but, honestly, it's not that *fauny*."

"Miles!"

"Okay, okay. The next thing that puzzled me was his unrelated medical issue. A heart problem. Really? In a healthy young man in prime shape? That's what really bothered me. I started checking all the records of young men that died recently. Miguel Ramos, Vernon Raincloud, and Tony Chow. These three also died of undiagnosed heart conditions, yet all three of them were in their prime. No indications of heart problems in their records."

Mercy bit her lip. "I missed all of that. A reaper doesn't usually focus on things like that. Our job is to get the person's spirit to its proper destination."

"I don't know if there is some magical being who is responsible for how and why people die—"

"There is," interrupted Mercy. "It is the Guardian of Death, but that Guardian has been missing for ten years. That's why it's so important that a replacement Guardian be found. Things like people dying for no reason shouldn't happen."

"Okay, makes sense. But as I was examining those who died, I noticed something even stranger."

Mercy looked at him questioningly. "Go on."

Miles hesitated. "I'm not really sure of this part, Mercy. It strikes me as the most bizarre thing I discovered." Mercy gave him a look of exasperation, then gestured for him to continue. Miles continued, "At about the same time that each of these four men died, someone else, who was listed in critical condition, suddenly recovered. Not just recovered but recovered enough to be returned to active duty."

Mercy realized that he was referring to the same men she had confronted Dr. Winters about. "You mean like Tony Ban."

Miles nodded. "Yes. He recovered at almost the exact moment that Ramos died. Danny Moore, who was in a coma and on a respirator as well as a heart pump, recovered at the same time that Gawain died. How is that possible? And the same was true for the other two individuals I discovered. What's going on, Mercy? The more I dug, the more I was convinced that Gini Brown was right. Something is going on at the Veteran's Hospital that isn't exactly kosher."

"Do you suspect one of the doctors at the Hospital?"

Miles smiled. "Now you're thinking like a homicide detective. Yes, I did, and still do."

"Which one?"

"It turns out that Doctor Cornel was the doctor in charge of two of the patients who died, and Doctor Sharpe was in charge of the other two. But only one doctor was involved with all four patients, though he was never the main physician in charge. Dr. Winters."

"So you think he was responsible?"

Miles sighed deeply. "Yes...and no. I think he was the instrument of what happened, though for the life of me, I cannot tell what it was that he did. But I think he was working with someone else."

"Who?"

"I don't know. But when I went to interview Dr Winters, he was talking with a man who had seven chakras lit up with nine shades of light and shadow. I'm told that's really rare. But I'm also told that such a person could perform all sorts of magic. I actually think that person was responsible for the sudden death-recovery switches."

"You didn't see his face?"

"I didn't even have a clear view of his back. I was still new to seeing chakras, and it was hard for me to focus on the soul-lights and the physical form at the same time. It's like near and far vision, I have to choose which one I want sharp and which blurry." He took a sip of orange juice. "Mercy, I don't want to put you in danger, but, could you do something for me?"

"I'm a Valkyrie, a Demi-Goddess of War... I'm not afraid of a little danger," she said. "How can I help?"

"Could you look out for pairs of patients that fit the pattern? A strong, healthy patient with a minor injury nearly ready for release, and a desperately ill, weak patient? I want to be ready if our perp strikes again."

"I can do that... hmm, Corey Ming is almost ready for release... he had his appendix removed. As for desperate patients..."

Mercy's alarm started beeping. "Oh, I have to leave now, or I won't make it to the hospital on time. But we *are* meeting Saturday, right?"

"I wouldn't miss it."

~

July 16, Saturday Evening

Mercy waited for Miles at the restaurant *The Woodland Grill.*

He didn't show up at 8 o'clock, as they agreed.

Maybe he's just running late.

She called his phone. It went to voicemail. She sent a text. No reply.

Half an hour crawled by.

Maybe I should listen to my mother and settle down with a nice reaper boy. Or a reaped Warrior.

The waiter asked if she was ready to order. She ordered an appetizer.

Another half an hour passed. If he showed now, he'd be an hour late...

She finished her appetizer alone. She ordered a soft drink. When she had to go to the ladies' room, she asked a waitress to keep an eye out in case her late date showed, and the waitress looked at her with pity.

Mercy returned to sit at the table alone.

The reaper got ghosted, she thought. It was the kind of joke Miles might have made.

She had a sudden urge to call her sister, Maven. They used to share all the ups and downs of their dates. But making a call to another Sphere... it wasn't just expensive, it was prohibitive.

A powerful wave of homesickness washed over her.

She had really hoped... but it looked like another guy couldn't handle either one part of her life or the other. And he hadn't even had the courtesy to call and say why.

After two hours, she left. She hadn't even ordered dinner.

At home, she ate ice cream. The cold lumps slid down her throat and refused to melt in her tummy. She kept eating until she felt sick.

Maybe he has a good reason, she thought. The compassionate nurse in her worried about him. *Maybe he's lying in a ditch somewhere, dying.*

And the Valkyrie part of her added, *That* better *be his excuse!*

~

July 16, Saturday Evening
Three Hours Earlier

Miles had just left his apartment when a dark-winged angel flew down and landed between him and his car.

"Miles Malone," intoned the dark angel. "I am here to kill you."

"It's really not a good time," said Miles. "Maybe we could postpone until tomorrow? I have a big date tonight."

"I don't know how you survived my last attempt to kill you," continued the dark angel. "But this time, there will be no loose ends. I won't do it here. I don't want to make a mess where it will upset the humans."

"And that's very considerate of you," said Miles, "But..."

The dark angel rushed at him, clawing him into the air as would a great raptor, and then vanishing into a tear in space-time.

For a moment there was a horrifying moment of pure nothing, and then space and time seem to tear open once again, with whiff of sulfur, and the raven-winged angel dropped Miles on the snowy, rocky ground of a mountain slope. Bitter wind howled, instantly stealing the warmth from Miles's body.

"Did you take me to the fabled world of eternal winter?" Miles asked, looking around the bleak snowy night landscape. "Or to hell itself?"

"You're still in the Rocky Mountains," said the angel.

It was then that Miles noticed a yellow bulldozer at the edge of the field. He realized he was on the edge of the construction site on Devil's Peak.

Miles lifted himself off his knees and stood on his feet to look his enemy in the face. That face was handsome and haunted and somewhat familiar, although much gaunter than the last photo that Miles had seen online.

And all of the angel's chakras were lit up like search lights.

The dark angel was holding two staves in one hand and supported some kind of wriggling animal in the crook of his other arm; it was a huge, tusked, horned pig.

"Judge Renaci?" Miles ventured. "Or should I call you Raziel? How about Raz? Why do you want to kill me? And why are you holding a pig?"

Raziel set the pig down.

"My name doesn't matter," rasped Raziel. "I've lost the right to any name."

Raziel threw Miles a staff and kept the other for himself. "I cannot kill an unarmed man. You can fight for your life."

"Yeah, wasn't I armed with a *gun* last time? I shot you point at point-blank range six times and then you shot of fireball at me. I don't think a stick is going to do me much good."

"I'm very sorry to slay you," Raziel said—and he did sound really bummed about it. "But if I don't kill you, they will kill the pig."

The pig snorted and started poking at the dirt with its snout.

"I vote for the pig," said Miles.

The dark angel smiled sardonically. "And you would probably be right to do so. The pig was not a very good man, even when he was a man."

The pig honked indignantly.

"You know it's true, Vass," said Raziel. "But he's still my only friend, and I will not see him killed, even if I must debase my own soul to protect him."

The pig ran to Raziel and butted his head against his shin. Raziel kicked him away. "Not now, Vass."

"Yeah," said Miles. "I can see you two are real close. So, have you been planning my murder for a long time, or did you just *wing* it?"

The angel bowed to him and waited for Miles to halfheartedly bow in return.

Then the angel shouted, "Fight!"

And launched himself at Miles.

Miles had fought criminals before. He was trained in several martial arts as well as regular police tactics, and he kept himself physically fit. But fighting the dark angel was like taking on a fireball inside a hurricane.

Miles stumbled backwards, using his agility to stay out of the way of his enemy's weapon as best he could. Raziel twirled his staff supernaturally fast, yet he took slow steps toward Miles.

"I'm going to do several things to your body to ensure that you die this time," Raziel explained remorsefully. "I'm going to chop off your head, and probably dice the rest of your limbs into small pieces. Then I might smash the pieces, to ensure the bones are broken. I might continue to pulverize them into a foamy mush. Then I'll most likely burn the whole pottage, in the interest of tidying up, really, because there should be no chance of you not thoroughly dying by that point.

"But don't worry, because before I do any of that, I will deliver one quick swift blow that will kill you instantly and painlessly, so you won't suffer any longer than necessary."

The dark angel's confidence was insulting, but Miles would take any advantage he could.

"So what's your favorite font?" asked Miles. "Let me guess, it's a *seraph* font."

Raziel stalked closer, whirling his staff. "You should focus on your defense, not on your jokes."

"I was hoping you'd die laughing," said Miles, "But maybe you don't get my humor... you're just an obtuse angel."

The pig rolled over on its back, snorting and kicking its hooved feet in the air.

"Really?" Raziel demanded, apparently addressing the pig. "You've not helping."

Miles took advantage of Raziel's distraction to shove the butt of his staff upwards into Raziel's throat.

Against any human, it would have been a killing blow.

But Raziel disappeared in a blast of dark smoke that stank like rotten eggs and reappeared behind Miles, delivering two sharp blows to his tailbone and knees. Paralyzed by agony, Miles toppled to the ice hardened ground.

Raziel strolled in a circle around Miles.

"Just tell me one thing before you kill me, Raz," grated Miles, his teeth clenched against the pain. "You can be honest with me since I'm about to die. Did you massacre the Guardians? You have enough magic that you could've done it, don't you? And I don't know what your damage is, but you obviously have a lot of issues..."

"Look on the bright side, Miles," the dark angel smiled grimly.

"When you leave this place, you're going someplace better. When I leave here, I'm going someplace worse. Whatever punishment you might wish upon me for doing this to you, know that it will surely happen."

"I'd rather..."

Raziel smashed his staff into Miles's head.

Eighteen

July 18, Monday

ON MONDAY MORNING, when Mercy cycled by his apartment, Miles wasn't sitting on his balcony, waiting to wave to her or invite her for orange juice and a bagel. It irked her that not only had he stood her up, now he didn't even dare show his face.

She peddled harder.

Some stubborn part of her hoped she'd see him at the hospital, poking around, asking questions. But Miles Malone hadn't shown up at the hospital either.

Maybe she ought to do some of her own poking around! Starting with finding out whether the "miracle" jewels that Winters was secretly passing to Cornel were really from the base.

Remembering how Dr Warren Winters had been lurking in the parking lot to meet a van, Mercy decided to lurk there again. Her hunch paid off when an unmarked, windowless van arrived. It was greeted by Winters.

This time, Mercy made certain to stay out of sight—she switched to her Valkyrie form, which, while normally much more flamboyant, she could also choose to make invisible and inaudible. After all, Valkyries often had to fly over battlefields, and they didn't like to become the targets of arrows, cannonballs, or guided missiles, in mundane battles, or attacked by Harpies, spells, or balls of hellfire on arcane battlefields.

The men who unloaded the van weren't in uniform, but they were strong, hefty men who could well have been soldiers. Three of them carried in boxes, following Winters into the hospital.

Mercy flew behind them, out of sight.

Winters had them bring the boxes all the way into his office. He opened a concealed door, revealing a storage space behind a bland wall. The men put down the new boxes and carried out the three boxes already in the office.

Hmm. It certainly did look like a delivery.

The delivery men departed immediately with their new loads, but Winters closed the concealed panels and sat at his desk.

She really wanted a peek in that closet. She flew back down to the nursing station, resumed her human form, and asked the nurse at the desk, "Could you page Dr Winters on behalf of nurse Beverly?"

Please forgive me for dragging you into this, Beverly, Mercy thought.

When the page went over the hospital intercom, Mercy flew back to Winter's office. As soon as he left, grumbling, she flew inside. She opened the panel, as she had seen him do, and she examined the contents of the boxes. She expected the new arrivals to be three boxes of glittering red jewels.

But when she opened the boxes, the jewels inside were clear as glass. The "substrate" hadn't been "charged" yet.

She touched the substrate, trying to figure out what kind of mineral it was. Plastic? Rock? Transparent aluminum? She couldn't tell by touching one. It was duller than diamond, and felt strangely light, which made her think of plastic, but it was incredibly clear, too clean to be a mundane material. Magic hummed in the object, even in its "uncharged" state.

Mercy frowned. If these were "empty," why had they just been delivered? Where did the "full" jewels come from and what filled them?

She pocketed one, then rearranged the rows to hide the theft. Winters would eventually know he was robbed, but she needed more information.

~

July 19, Tuesday

Miles woke up, cold and aching all over. If he had to describe the feeling, he would've said it felt as if he had been beaten with a stick, diced up into pieces, pulverized, set on fire, and then frozen again.

But that was probably just his imagination playing games with him. That couldn't possibly have happened, or he wouldn't have woken up, still alive on the mountain. Obviously, everything the raven-winged man had said was to intimidate him.

Then again, Miles *was* stark naked, and lying in a pile of burnt ground.

It was daylight. Miles estimated the temperature was above zero, but given the thin air, the elevation must have been high enough that it would plunge back down quickly.

He stood up and started shuffling forward. After what felt like an eternity of walking, he turned around to see how far he had come. He was dismayed to see it was only about ten yards. His gaze drifted across the field and landed on the bulldozer.

He wondered if there was any chance someone might have left the keys in it. Did bulldozers have keys? He was about to find out.

Maybe he should also try to figure out why people kept trying to kill him.

And maybe he should ask himself why it didn't seem to work.

And maybe he should also figure out what he was going to tell Mercy when he called her to apologize for missing their date.

He couldn't tell her that he had been killed but then came back to life. Even to an arcane, that would sound crazy. Plus, Miles didn't want to think about what her response as a reaper might be. She might find it personally offensive that his body, for some reason, refused to die.

~

July 19, Tuesday

Again, on Tuesday, when Mercy cycled by Miles's apartment, the balcony was empty. He was definitely avoiding her.

Miles didn't even bother to call. When her phone flashed his name, when he finally did call, she wondered if she should even pick it up. Maybe she should just text him that it was over, since he obviously didn't mean enough to her to even cancel a date properly when he couldn't make it.

But on the third ring, she gave in and answered the phone.

"Mercy? This is Miles. Remember me? You might not. In fact, it might be better if you just assume this call is from a complete stranger, someone who never did something incredibly stupid, like make a date with you, and then not show up. Because a guy like that, you probably wouldn't want to see again. But a guy like me, a handsome, incognito stranger, who just happens to also want to go on a date with you, *and will definitely not stand you up this time*—maybe you would give a guy like that a chance?"

"What happened?" she asked.

"I got held up," he said. "Somebody really wanted a meeting with me, and he insisted on having our tete-a-tete on Devil's Mountain... you know, where the construction site is? It took forever, and he left me there without a ride home. At the end of the meeting, I was dead tired, absolutely fried."

"And you didn't have your phone?"

"Funny story. Apparently, I dropped it on the way up the mountain. In fact, I had to buy a new phone. They gave me the old number though. The first thing I did on my new phone was call you. How about we try again? This Friday?"

She was about to say that she couldn't, because she always had dinner with her family on Friday, but then she thought, if he stood her up again, at least this time she would have someplace to go afterward to commiserate.

"Okay," she said. "But I don't know if I'm going to bother to put on make-up on this time. It's a lot of effort you know."

"That's fine, since I'm the one who should be making up to you," he said.

She laughed, despite herself. "Okay, Miles. Second chance. Don't blow it this time."

~

July 20, Wednesday

This time nothing will stop our date, Mercy promised herself.

It was only after Sumiko the Shinigami called Mercy and left a message on her phone saying how much she was looking forward to seeing her at the Reapers Conference that Mercy suddenly remembered she had a prior engagement.

Oh, no! How could I have forgotten the Reapers Conference?! She had been only been looking forward to it *for the last six months!* She had signed on to get the early bird pricing. And now she had almost forgotten it started this Friday! How could her date with a man who stood her up, a man she shouldn't have been dating in the first place, have erased such an important event from her mind?

Reluctantly, she called Miles.

"I'm so sorry, she said. "I was really looking forward to our date tonight. I totally forgot I had signed up for a conference this weekend."

There was a pause in which all she could hear was the beating of her heart.

"I understand," he said. He didn't push her on it, but she could tell that he thought she was blowing him off.

"Maybe another time," he said, not pressing her for a day, time, or place. He was giving her an easy out. As if he strongly doubted they would date again, he added, "I'm sure I'll see you around town. We can work something out if it happens. If not, it's no big deal."

But it was a big deal to her. She was not trying to give him the brush off and she wanted him to know it.

"It's too bad you can't come with me," she said. "I mean, it's right here in Arcana Glen, and they usually sell tickets at the door..."

"Would you want me there? What kind of conference is it?"

"It's a business convention for me, but tourists who are interested in the industry also come to see the booths and the merchandise."

"What industry? Medicine? Or your *other* calling...? Wait, do *reapers* have conventions?"

"Why not?"

"Sure, why not. It's very interesting that there's a reapers convention in town this weekend. That... amazing. Mercy, I would consider it a favor from you if you *would* invite me to this. I can find out the answer to questions I've always wanted to ask the Grim Reaper. What kind of music do reapers prefer? Death metal or soul? What's a reaper's favorite Christmas movie? Die Hard?"

Mercy giggled. "Are you even taking this seriously?"

"I am, I assure you," he said, more somberly. "If you don't mind if I do a little research on the case while I'm there. I'm sorry for being so obsessed with my work..."

"No, on the contrary, I feel better about it if I know you aren't just wasting money to spend time with me at a boring conference. If you think it can actually help you on your case, that's great. We'll both get something out of it. I don't really see how it will help you though."

"An entire convention of soul reapers is in town, and you don't think that will be relevant to investigating a serial killer?"

"You don't think a reaper could be responsible, do you?"

"Is it possible? Magically, I mean."

Mercy fell silent. He was right, but she didn't want to admit it. Reapers worked so hard to combat the prejudice that they KILLED the people whose souls they reaped—that a reaper could decide whether an individual lived or died but just wanted people to die. That wasn't the case at all. Yet, a reaper did *have the ability* to abuse their power.

"It's...possible," she finally admitted. "But I can't imagine any reaper doing that. It would be incredibly unprofessional."

"It would be unprofessional for a doctor to murder his patients, too."

"Uh... good point. Does that mean you suspect me too?" she teased.

Miles laughed dryly. "I'm a suspicious guy. I suspect everyone."

"As it happens, I'm on your side and I did some snooping of my own. I have something to tell you that I think might be related to the case," Mercy said. "But I'd rather tell you in person."

"What time do you want me to pick you up to go to the conference?" he asked. "Maybe we should try to get there early, so I can buy a ticket before they run out."

"I doubt they'll run out but that's still a good idea."

After she hung up, she thought about what a strange Hourglass Miles had and how other reapers might be... excessively curious about it. She needed some way to protect him.

There was a jewelry store, *The Crystal Emporium* in Arcana Glen, run by a hoary family of Stone Witches, the Silvers, renowned for selling magic gems. Perhaps she would find something there. While she was there, she would ask about the Miracle Jewel. If anyone would know crystal magic, the Silver family would.

July 21, Thursday Morning

Early on Thursday, Miles called Maverick Cade.

"Hey, you said you'd be willing to help me with any computer stuff."

"That's right."

"Would you be able to get me personnel records of the military base near Arcana Glen?"

A long pause. Then: "Yes."

"I'd like to know about transfers of personnel to the base from the hospital, and perhaps vice versa," said Miles. "Going back as far as possible. Also, access to medical records sealed by the military. I don't know if you can get all that..."

"I can get it," said Mavrick. He hung up without saying goodbye.

July 21, Thursday Evening

Mercy dropped by *The Crystal Emporium* after work. A pert young woman, with dark skin that humans probably mistook for a shade of brown, but was actually a shade of earthy-green, greeted her. Clearly, a

Stone Witch, with a mix of human and Autumn Elf ancestry, her name tag identified her as a manager named Roki Silver.

Roki tipped back her white, rhinestone cowboy hat and flashed a smile. "How can I help you?"

"I'm looking for a Shield ring," Mercy said.

"What price range?"

"The best you have, the price doesn't matter," shrugged Mercy.

Roki's grin grew wider. "You're my favorite kind of customer. I can show you some fine pieces that we keep in the back. For you?"

"No... for a friend of mine... a man."

"I'm going to need his ring size."

"I can estimate, I think. I need it by tomorrow, so if I have to buy one a bit loose, that's fine. He can have it resized later."

Roki took Mercy into a private salon at the back of the store, where the truly fine pieces were shown privately to the most exclusive clientele. While looking over the selection of men's rings, Mercy broached the other issue.

"I was wondering if you could help me with something else. A consultation on a gem I have... if I need to pay for the consultation, I can..."

"If you want a piece evaluated, I can do that free of charge," said Roki. "May I see the gem?"

Mercy placed the white crystal on the velvet-topped table between them.

Roki reached out to touch the gem. Her fingernails were exquisitely painted, tipped with rhinestones. But when her fingertips came close to the clear gem, she yelped and yanked back her hand.

For the first time, Roki stared hard at Mercy with a flat, unfriendly glower.

"That's not a gemstone, first of all," said Roki. "It's not an earth rock, or any kind of mineral. It doesn't use Elemental Stone magic at all. It's a structure somehow created out of solidified air, using Elemental Wind magic. And Dark magic. It's *empty*. And *thirsty*. And *evil*. It's like a vampire in inanimate form. Where did you get this?"

Mercy stammered. She could hardly admit she stole it from a hospital. She mumbled some vague explanation, paid for the ring, and hurried out of the Emporium.

~

July 22, Friday

It was a busy weekend at the convention center of the hotel next to the casino. Three conventions were actually being held simultaneously, although only one was arcane. Mercy felt as if she had flown a thousand miles to the special New World just because she was going to be meeting reapers from all over the spheres and because Miles was accompanying her. Her whole body tingled with nervous excitement. She was anxious that he have a good time, and worried that he would find it incredibly boring or even creepy. She didn't think there was anything creepy about her profession, but she knew most mundanes found it so.

There were two lines, one for those who already had tickets and one line for those who had to purchase tickets. Those who already had tickets could basically simply enter the main doors of the convention hall. But those who had to buy tickets had to wait in line at a kiosk in the atrium of the hotel. Mercy naturally waited with Miles.

"Can you tell that everyone waiting in line is arcane?" she asked him in a whisper.

"I think so." He didn't whisper but he did keep his voice low. "They have their traffic lights turned on."

"That's..." She wrinkled her for head.

He chuckled. "That's my own private description. The books I got told me that it means that the chakras are open. At least one or two of them. That seems to be the main difference between arcanes and mundanes, as far as I can tell."

"Oh. I can't even tell. I don't even know what a chakra looks like."

"How can you tell arcanes from mundanes?"

"To be honest, I often can't. What I look at is how much life force they have. Usually, arcanes have a stronger or longer life force. More sand in the hourglass, that's how it looks to me. But sometimes there are other things I can see."

She tapped the tips of her ears and the canines of her teeth, indicating the two most obvious things about Elves and Shifters. She could look at the teeth of a shifter in human form and tell (usually) what kind of animal person became. And Elves were obvious because of their ears, large jewel-bright eyes, and colorful hair. Although come to think of it, so many humans dyed their hair strange colors that wasn't even an obvious tell anymore.

"It's funny," she said, "I never thought about it before, but I don't think the difference between people from different Spheres matters as much to us reapers as it does to other types. To us, the one thing all mortals have in common is that everyone dies."

"Even Elves?"

"Oh yes. They have long life spans, but they are mortal."

"But what about angels and demons?"

"Yes, even them. Except beings who directly come from the Last Home as messengers, the true Angels you might say, in the sense of being holy beings—not just powerful beings. All the rest of us are mortal. Demons have horns and wings, angels have wings and are surrounded by halos of light, and they all have powers that look like magic to ordinary humans, but most of them are mortals like Shifters and Elves."

"Are there some angels which are also reapers? Dark-winged angels, maybe..."

"Wing color has nothing to do with it. Technically, any being born in Dayhaven is an 'angel' with a lower-case 'A.' I'm technically an angel. So, yes, most reapers are either some species of angel or demon. It requires a certain level of power that other beings don't have."

"So there is a hierarchy of power."

Mercy shrugged. "To a reaper, every creature born in the lower Seven Spheres looks the same. Everyone dies and must be judged before they can go onto the Last Home. Some souls are reincarnated in different Spheres first, but the final destination is always the same."

"What happens if someone should die... But they don't?"

"That would be very bad. Some creatures do try to escape death. Usually through dark magic twisted to an evil purpose. Not all dark magic has to be evil, please understand that. But it can be twisted. The natural law can be broken. For a time. The consequences are so dire that every reaper in existence would soon try to stop such a person."

"I see." He glanced away from her. "This line sure is moving slowly. Maybe I should just let you go in. I could go home and return when you called to pick you up and drive you home. You shouldn't have to wait around for me."

"Oh," she said, "It's no problem. It's so much more fun going to a convention with somebody than by yourself. It's like eating in a restaurant alone."

A smile bent his lips. "That, I can understand. Okay, Mercy. I'll stay. I just hope I don't cause you any trouble."

That tickled her memory. "I almost forgot!" She dug into her purse. "I brought a present for you."

Shyly, she handed him a tiny box.

Miles quirked his eyebrow. "It looks like a jewelry box."

"It's a ring."

"Uh... aren't I the one who's supposed to go down on one knee, then pop open a box with a ring in it...?"

"Not that kind of ring, silly." She grinned. She held up her right hand, showing him a gold and black ring on her index finger. The gemstone was deep black but deep within its inky depths, flecks of gold and blue shimmered. "It's a Privacy Ring, with an enchanted Nuummite gemstone. Wear it on your right hand, on Mr. Pointy."

"'*Mr. Pointy*?'" he echoed. The ring was a fat, masculine version of her own, with the same depths, like a pool of black oil swimming with gold and sapphire fish deep within. Miles looked stunned. "This is a gorgeous ring, Mercy. I'll return it at the end of the convention."

"It's a gift. Keep it. I had it made for you."

He slipped the ring on his right index finger.

"It fits!" Mercy said.

"Perfectly. It's a kingly gift, and very thoughtful. Thank you, Mercy."

"Don't take it off, okay? Not even in the bathroom."

"Afraid I'll put it down next to the sink and forget it? Don't worry, I would never lose a gift from you."

Nineteen

July 22, Friday

MILES COULD TELL that if he had seen this crowd waiting in line at the convention even just a week ago, before his new abilities had kicked in so mysteriously, he would've had no clue any of these people were anything other than a bunch of boring professionals, at a typical middle management trade show and job fair. They looked like they were here for a dentist convention, not a Death convention.

When Miles and Mercy finally reached the kiosk where he bought his ticket, it was just like any other convention. He handed over his credit card; a bored looking Elf ran it through the card reader and handed Miles a plastic lanyard with his name and title—in this case it just said "guest"—and a folder containing a schedule of events and several brochures for tools evidently aimed at reapers. Who knew that there was an entire sub industry peddling tools of the trade to Grim Reapers?

"This is excellent," he told Mercy. "I've been wondering where to buy a new scythe."

"Oh, don't use that brand," she said glancing at the brochure. "They're terribly overpriced."

"But I wouldn't want to get a cheap one. My last one broke. Of course, that might've been because I also tried to use it to cut weeds."

She finally realized he was teasing her. She hit him with the back of her hand, playfully, and they went into the convention hall.

"You may think it's funny," she said as he took in the huge convention hall filled with booth after booth of reaper-related material, "but a good scythe can be useful. Sometimes the soul doesn't want to completely let go of the body, and the 'stem,' so to speak, kind of 'sticks' to the corpse. Then you take your scythe and *BAM!* you free the soul from the body."

"Do you have a scythe?"

"No, I have a spear, but I don't usually have to use it on the souls I'm reaping," she admitted. "Remember, most of the people I am taking *want* to come. Not that they want to die, exactly. It's important to my job that they fight to live, it's a whole thing where I can't take them if they *try* to die…"

Miles scratched his head, exaggerating his confusion. "Let me get this straight. You only take people who want to die, but if they want to die then you can't take them? Yeah, that's perfectly clear." He broke into a broad smile.

"It's not funny!" she said, laughing. "I'm trying to explain it, but how can I when you're making those silly faces at me?"

"Come on, Mercy, it's just death, don't take it so seriously." He made a silly face. "If you can't joke about death, what can you joke about? I loaded up on more reaper jokes just for this convention."

"Miles!" she giggled.

"How does a reaper keep his cloak so black?"

"Uh…"

"With *dye*."

"Are you going to keep telling jokes the whole weekend?" she demanded, trying to suppress her giggles.

"I'm just trying to fit in with some *killer* humor."

"Don't let anyone else hear you mocking our profession!" She wagged her finger at him, trying and failing to suppress her smile. "We are very serious people!"

"Why can't I tell jokes? Will there be *reaper-cussions?*"

She groaned.

Miles leaned close to her and murmured in her ear, "Why are reapers so sexy?"

"What?!" she gasped. His breath against her neck sent delicious tingles down her spine.

"They're *breathtaking*." He winked at her. "Or maybe that's just you."

Mercy flushed shell pink, and stepped back, suddenly wide-eyed and shy.

"Okay, okay," Miles said, holding his hands up in surrender, still with a twinkle of amusement in his eye, "I'm going to take this completely seriously now. Let's take a look at the schedule and see what we should do first."

He perused his schedule, then peered over the paper.

"It looks like reapers specialize in different kinds of deaths. *'Drowning Today.'* That sounds good—I'm eager to dive into that topic. *'Cancer Deaths: Preparing for the Upcoming Boom.'* I'm glad to see someone is looking on the dynamite side of cancer, it's usually such a downer topic. This one is interesting. *'When Your Disease has been Eradicated: Steps for Next Moves in a Disease Reaping Career.'* Oh good, I would hate to think that researchers coming up with medical miracles might put reapers out of business. Is this really how it works? Different reapers for different kinds of deaths?"

"In general," she said still snickering at his tone of voice reading the headlines from the program schedule. "Some are actually more related to the kind of life that the person lived, like my work for instance."

"Is there a reaper for Dying of Embarrassment? Is that a thing? I mean every teenager says they're going to die of embarrassment about fifty times a day, but how many of them really follow through?"

"This is the one I want to go to," she said growing a little more serious. She pointed to the headline speech. "*'Ghost Overpopulation: Is there a Solution on the Horizon?'*"

"Ghost overpopulation." Miles raised his eyebrows. "That's a new one to me."

"It's very serious," she said. "Normally, there are enough people who can travel through the Gates on their own that the reapers can handle the special cases. That's why so many of the reapers you see giving speeches are for the more gruesome or unexpected forms of death. Those are usually the kinds of people who need help dealing with their unexpected post-life state. The rest can usually find their own Door automatically. But ever since the Massacre of the Guardians... yes," she said in response to his startled look, "the same Massacre that the Magician asked you to help him find out more about...anyway, ever since then, there has been no Guardian of Death. The Guardian of Death is kind of like the head reaper."

"Why don't they choose a new one?"

"They are trying to. I don't exactly know what the criteria are myself though. Many reapers here would jump at the opportunity."

"Not you."

"I don't have a chance. I think, at the very least you have to prove that you're stronger than the other reapers."

"Stronger? How?"

Mercy hesitated. He could tell she was searching for words, so he did not pressure her. The whole time they had been speaking together, they'd been walking down the aisles of booths, and Miles was carefully observing everyone around him. It seemed to him that in here, unlike in the lobby of the hotel, many of the reapers were allowing themselves to show their true form. He saw women with the legs and wings of vultures; skeletons nine feet tall, ghostly people in white robes trailing into blood drenched hems. Glowing red eyes were popular. He saw a man with pins sticking out all over his body and face; creatures with mouths where their eyes should've been and eyes where their bellies should've been; creatures with tusks, fangs and teeth of all sorts. Even the pets people brought with them, and several did, looked horrifying. There were huge black dogs with flames for eyes and jowls that dripped something onto the carpet that caused it to hiss and smoke. There were three-headed dogs as well. He should've expected that, Miles thought. And he even saw a woman holding a horrible cat that looks like something out of a nightmare. Oops, no, those were ordinary hairless "Sphinx" cats.

It was as if every horror show from every October release of the past fifty years had come to life and bought a ticket to this convention.

"I found out from a friend recently what's required to become the Guardian of Death," continued Mercy, ignoring the hideous cat, which hissed at them as they passed it, "You have to prove you were strong enough that you could reap other reapers. You have to prove you could reap—if you needed to—*every other reaper*. Our contest of strength is very primordial, because ours is a very primal and archaic profession. Basically, you have to defeat other reapers in battle."

"Or maybe," Miles said, with a gesture, "You could just go ask the lady at that booth over there."

Mercy turned to see what he was pointing at. At the far end of the auditorium was a booth elevated on a dais. A long snaking line, divided by golden posts and red velvet ropes like the line at the bank, looped around and around, down the steps of the dais, and halfway around the wall of the auditorium. On the dais itself, an elaborate throne had been set up, rather like Santa's Throne at Christmastime, in front of a deep indigo curtain that hung between a black and a white pillar. A dark-haired woman with a veil over her face, a tiara of moonstones and a simple dress of deep blue and silver sat upon the throne. A little round table with a scroll of some sort sat before her. More curtains, translucent white, surrounded the entire set up. These did not conceal what happened at the table, but did obscure it, as if by a light mist.

Two attendants stood outside the translucent curtains. A towering man with a scythe, golden armor, white wings like feathers of silver fire, who was bathed in a radiant halo, stood at the top of the steps, guarding the crowned woman on one side of the dais. On the other side of the dais, at the entrance to the line, a blonde woman acted like a Santa's Helper Elf. It was she who allowed, one by one, those in line to ascend the steps to sit across from crowned dark-haired beauty at the table.

The sign over the mystic throne, arced like a rainbow over the two pillars, read:

CONSULT THE SEERESS –
FIND OUT IF YOU ARE THE NEXT GUARDIAN OF DEATH!

Twenty

July 23, Saturday

THE LINE TO see the Seeress was too long to try on Friday, the first night of the convention. However, on Saturday, Miles drove Mercy to the convention as soon as the doors opened.

"We have to compete with all those who slept in the hotel and only need to trot downstairs to get there," he said. "So I'll pick up breakfast to go and we'll eat in line. We'll get you in to see the Seeress before the line extends half-way around the hall."

Even with all that effort, the line still seemed too long to Mercy, but Miles said she ought to try.

"I really have no chance," she insisted. Especially, she thought, after seeing every other reaper at the convention, and possibly every reaper in the Seven Lower Spheres, queue up to audition with the Seeress.

"You don't know until you give it a shot," said Miles. "There's no failure except failing to try."

She groaned, but how could she refuse when he was so endearing to encourage her? It wasn't a hardship to wait in line when she could talk to him. Somehow, they never ran out of things to talk about. At first, she wondered if he was listening to her, because he constantly scanned the room around them, as if expecting something to happen. But he proved that he attended to every detail, not only by remembering what she said later but by asking insightful questions that made her think differently about issues she'd thought long settled.

"So you could never marry a human," he asked after she made a careless, throw-away remark. "Is it a species thing—you can't mate with a human? Or is it that humans aren't, uh, as evolved, or advanced as you? I mean, technically, from what I have gleaned, you *are* an angel, or even a demi-goddess, depending on how one labels the pantheon of higher beings."

"It's not either of those things," she said. "Yes, I could, ah, have children with a human. That's why there are Witches, Shifters, and sensitives in the human population—they are the descendants of mixed marriages. And I don't think I'm better than you. I never wanted to marry a human because it would be too hard to be myself. Even if I could reveal my Valkyrie side, it might, uh, frighten him off. It happened a couple of times when I first arrived in the Mundane Sphere and tried to date human men. Either they couldn't see my other form at all, or they ran away, screaming."

"I've seen you other form," said Miles. "I'm still here. Listen." He caressed her ear. "No screaming."

His gentle touch made her breathless. "No, you didn't run away screaming. I could see myself marrying a human if he was like you." She blushed and ducked her head. "Wow, this line is moving really slowly, isn't it?"

She needed to change the topic. "I found out something about the 'jewels' that Cornel mentioned."

Miles listened while she filled him in.

"I wish I knew more about magic," he frowned. "Wind magic, Stone magic, it's all hocus-pocus to me. Dark magic sounds bad, especially if you add, 'empty, thirsty, vampire in inanimate form,' to the description. What does it signify to you?"

"The Azir are involved."

"Another term I've never heard."

"The Winter Elves."

"Pale skin, white hair, pointy ears, jewel-like eyes?"

"You've met some, I see."

He made a joke of it. "We weren't formally introduced, but a few of them tried to kill me a while back. Fun times."

"What! Why didn't you tell me!"

"If you want to hear about it every time some magical being tries to kill me, we'd never have any chance to talk about you," said Miles. "I don't want to be a bore."

"Has anyone else tried to kill you?!"

"Recently? A dark-winged angel." He shrugged abashedly. "I didn't want to mention it, but that's where I was the night I was supposed to meet you. This angel who has a beef with me carried me to Devil's Peak and started whacking me with a stick."

"Miles, I can't believe you didn't tell me! Why would he do that?"

"He's an angel, I guess he just wanted to beat *the hell* out of me."

"On the contrary, he was probably working for Hell—for Darkpyre. Only a Fallen Angel would do something like that."

"I don't know if he was a Fallen Angel, but he was definitely a Maulin' Angel. He used to have a human cover, before he apparently blew it... Judge Raziel Renaci."

"By the Light! Judge Renaci!"

"You know him?"

"I know *of* him. He was so... respectable. I can't believe it!"

"See? You can't trust anybody. Was the judge known to have a pet pig?"

"Not that I know of, but I wasn't in his social circle. He was simply well known, and liked, around Arcana Glen. Considered very fair and above corruption."

"You know what they say. Lie down with pigs, you're going to wake up dirty."

When it was Mercy's turn at last, a pretty blonde woman with a cheerful smile pulled aside the velvet cord and allowed Mercy to cross the elevated platform and sit at the table across from the Seeress. At first, Mercy could hardly see the Seeress's face, because the veil that fell down from her moonstone tiara obscured her features. However, as the session began, the dark-haired Seeress lifted her veil and draped it back over her head. It had been fashioned with clever design so that it could hang in either direction without obscuring the crown she wore.

"I really like your crown," Mercy said. Then she wanted to kick herself. She was not here to make small talk with the third most powerful Guardian in the Seven Spheres.

The Seeress had a beautiful face, kind and gentle with dark violet luminous eyes.

"Thank you," she said softly. "Please give me your hand and I will try to do a reading."

Mercy held out her hands on the table palms facing up. "I'm sorry if they're sweaty," she said. "I'm really nervous."

"Before I touch you, I must warn you," the Seeress said, "by touching you, I will have a Vision that will tell me something about you. It may be a Vision from your past, it may be something about your present, it may be something about your future. I may see a Vision of your own death, even though you are a reaper yourself. I may see a dark secret that you have never wanted to share with anyone else. If you don't wish me to see something like this, this is your chance to walk away. No one will know what we talked about together, and no one will know if I saw or did not see any Vision about you. Please think about this for a moment in silence. When you are ready, if you are ready, then we will touch, and I will welcome the Vision that comes to me."

"I'm as ready as I'll ever be," said Mercy. "Let's just do it. I don't have any big secrets or a very interesting past."

The Seeress touched her hands. At once, the dark-haired woman's eyes rolled back into her head, making her eyeballs look completely white. Then her whole demeanor changed.

"I am Sabriel," she said in a voice that somehow seemed to be different than the voice she had used before. This voice was older, accented oddly, and more sardonic. "I am the High Priestess, the Queen of Swords, she who was murdered! I am the Seeress who was the Seeress before the Body whose hands you touch. *She* is not with us now. What I have to tell you, Mercy, is for your ears alone, because you alone can do what must be done. You *must* find the Rogue Immortal, the One who Evades Death. You must fight him. And you must reap his soul. You and you alone can do so. He is not who he appears. He is the one who will not die. He is the one who slew us all!"

Alarmed, Mercy tried to jerk her hands free, but the Seeress wouldn't let go.

"But I don't know who that is!" cried Mercy. "I want to help, I really do. I just don't know what you're talking about. And even if I could find him, I don't have the strength to take down someone who can evade other reapers!"

"You will know him because you will see him die and return to life right in front of you," declared Sabriel. Her voice became cold and foreboding. "If you do not stop the man who refuses to die, he will strike again and *all of the new Guardians will die!*"

All at once, the dark-haired woman jerked her hands free and collapsed on the table.

The blonde woman, who had been waiting outside the curtained area, rushed inside crying, "Kyrah! Are you okay?"

The dark-haired Seeress sat up straight again, rubbing her temples as if her head throbbed.

"Sabriel possessed me, Bethany," Kyrah told the blonde woman. "I recognized her energy, but... She took me over and locked me out. She's never done that before."

"How dare she!" exclaimed Bethany, very angry. "If she tries to do it again, I'll punch her in the face!"

"Please don't do that, Bethany," said Kyrah with a pained look. "Since it would be my actual face you would be punching."

"Oh, yeah. I forgot about that complication. Fine, I'll get Michael in here and have him attack her with his angel scythe. Michael!"

The blond warrior in golden armor entered the tent. It seemed strange to Mercy, but it was obvious that none of those outside the curtains had heard what was said inside. It must be magic, she thought because the wispy translucent curtains certainly would not keep out normal sound under ordinary circumstances.

The Seeress, Kyrah, addressed Mercy directly for the first time since she recovered herself. "What did Sabriel say to you?"

"The first thing she told me was that what she had to say was for my ears alone," said Mercy. "Should I still tell you? Is Sabriel a bad person?"

"She's a spirit," said Kyrah, "Being the spirit of the last Seeress before me, apparently, she can still visit the Mundane Sphere when she wishes. And she can be quite intense. Her message to you must have been most urgent if she took over my body without allowing me to hear what was said between the two of you. But if she told you the message was for you alone... Michael, what do you think?"

"We are only here to answer one question," he said, turning to Mercy, "Did she tell you that you are the next Guardian of Death? If she did, then you should tell us that, even if she asked you not to."

"No, she didn't say anything like that."

"In that case, whatever she had to say was undoubtedly a private message to you from someone in the Last Home. Perhaps even the most important someone. Guard the message carefully and treat it as a treasure."

"Should I obey it?"

"It was an injunction?" Michael asked.

"Yes. She said there would be dire consequences if I didn't do it."

"Then indeed, you should do it. Or not. I cannot judge. You should always remember that you never *have* to use a medium to get a message. If you are uncertain, you can always ask the Light yourself for advice. Never do anything that violates your own conscience. But if your conscience tells you that the injunction was good and necessary, then you should listen."

"Thanks, I guess." Mercy frowned. This was not turning out at all as she had hoped.

Misunderstanding her dismay, the Kyrah said softly, "I'm sorry if you didn't get the news you wanted to hear about becoming the next Guardian of Death."

"It's not that," said Mercy. "I never expected that, to be honest. It's just that... I think I was told to do something really important that I'm not able to do. I'm not strong enough."

"You can ask us for help if you need it," said Bethany.

Mercy blinked. The way the blonde woman included herself in with the other two Guardians indicated she was probably a Guardian herself. Mercy had somehow assumed she was only an assistant, perhaps because of her somewhat haphazard mannerisms and goofy smile.

"Thank you, *Sarmateem*," she said gravely, bowing to all three of them. "I think it's something I'm supposed to figure out on my own."

Twenty-One

July 23, Saturday

AFTER HER SESSION with the Seeress, Mercy returned to where Miles waited. He had been leaning against the wall, observing the reapers at the conference with an air of fascination. He straightened when he saw her.

"Were you bored while I was gone?" asked Mercy.

"Nope. I was able to get some work done," said Miles. "I called I guy I played a video game with and he updated me the miraculously recovered patients who went on to work at the military base."

Mercy was interested in hearing more, but Miles asked, "So are you the new Lady Death?"

She shook her head. "Nope. Still just a regular reaper."

"Disappointed or relieved?" he asked.

"A little of both, I guess." She shrugged. "But not exactly surprised. We have some time before the Keynote Address. Do you mind if we do a little shopping?"

"Not at all."

They strolled through the maze of booths in the main room. Many of the stalls sold various items useful to reapers, such as stones and gems, specialized weapons, and even physical hourglasses that you could attune to different souls so you could monitor many souls at the same time, even if you weren't standing right in front of them. Her budget didn't allow her to buy everything that caused her to squeal in delight. She lingered for a long time over an ancient, enchanted Viking scythe in pristine condition. But in the end, she decided it was an unnecessary indulgence. The vendor, a Skelly reaper, did his best to persuade her, but she forced herself to walk away.

She didn't want to miss the Keynote Address on Ghost Overpopulation. In order to get a seat in the main auditorium, which was filling up fast, Miles suggested that they grab chairs early.

The speaker before the Keynote Address was a reaper of those who died during meals or due to complications from overeating. He was also there to talk up the Keynote Speaker.

This was a rather sensitive topic to Mercy, since unfortunately, being a reaper did not make her immune to the kinds of foibles that doomed mortals to an early death. She knew that overindulgence was a particular weakness of hers.

"This is a huge field," the speaker began, "and it's only growing. We need more reapers to come into the field of reaping obesity-related deaths because it's only going to get fatter as the years go by." He laughed heartily at his own joke.

"That's worse than my jokes," muttered Miles.

It didn't help when, only minutes into the reaper's bombastic speech, Miles whispered to Mercy, "I will be right back. I have to go visit the little boy's room."

She had been about to use the same excuse to get away, but he had beat her to it. She nodded and grimaced. Someone had to stay and save their seats. While there was honor among reapers, the seats were indeed filling up fast just as Miles had predicted and she didn't trust some of the reapers around her. The Harpy at the end of the aisle had just tossed aside someone else's sweater and snatched the seat for herself. Not ten minutes later one of her girlfriends, another Harpy, arrived and did the same to the purse in the next seat over. And in fact, the Harpy even went through the purse and picked money out of the wallet. Outrageous!

She hoped Miles would get back soon. Without him, it hit her how boring the convention was. When he was around, everything was a source of endless discussion and terrible puns. He made everything better.

❧

Miles had been wondering what he could do to thank Mercy for bringing him to the convention. And... The truth was he just wanted to buy her a present. He had observed her carefully while she was looking at the sales booths, taking careful note of which items she truly wanted but talked herself out of. Based on how long she lingered over it, he thought that what she truly wanted was the large Viking style scythe she had sighed over and caressed.

That made sense. It wasn't really a "Viking" scythe, but a scythe forged in Valhalla, her homeland, she had told him. He had expressed surprise she didn't already have one. She told him it was traditional, and she kept thinking she should get one to complete her Valkyrie outfit, but she could never bring herself to invest the money.

Looking at the price tag on the scythe, Miles could see why. It cost as much as a high-quality gun. Still, you should expect to invest in a good weapon, whether it was mystical and decorative or modern and actually useful.

After so many months of being tight on funds himself, it felt odd to be able to splurge. He was glad that his work for the Magician had resulted in him having extra funds for once. He would not have been able to buy this gift if he were still worried about paying his secretary or his mortgage.

But then he ran into a little snag. He saw the seller taking the scythe off of the long handle and putting it by itself into a box.

"What are you doing?" Miles asked. "I need the handle too."

"That costs more," said the vendor. He named a price.

"That's almost as much is the scythe!"

"Half the magic is in the handle," said the vendor. "The handle charges the weapon between uses. It also sharpens it automatically. So it's *worth* almost as much as the scythe itself."

Milo's shoulders sagged. He wanted to get Mercy the perfect present but getting a scythe with no handle seemed like a bad gift. It was almost worse than getting no scythe at all.

The vendor apparently saw his dilemma.

"Look," said the man. Actually, he wasn't a man, he was a skeleton, but his bony skull was surprisingly expressive for someone with no muscles or skin. "I'll cut you a deal. I see that you're wearing a Shield ring. If you trade that to me, I'll give you the handle with the scythe."

Miles was surprised. "This ring is worth as much is that?"

Now he had a dilemma. Mercy had told him it was a gift and that he could keep it, but did that mean she would be offended if he traded it? He decided that if it was really a gift to him, then he would gladly trade it to return a gift to her.

"Deal," he said. He removed the ring and handed it over to the skeleton. The skeleton attached the handle to the scythe, and then wrapped the whole weapon an a very fine box. The skeleton handed the gift set over to Miles.

Miles handed over the Nuumite ring. The skeleton, took it, murmuring thanks to Miles... Then his skull sockets widened in shock.

"Is anything wrong? Miles asked.

"No..." stammered the skeleton. "You just have a very unusual aura."

I wonder what the hell that means, thought Miles.

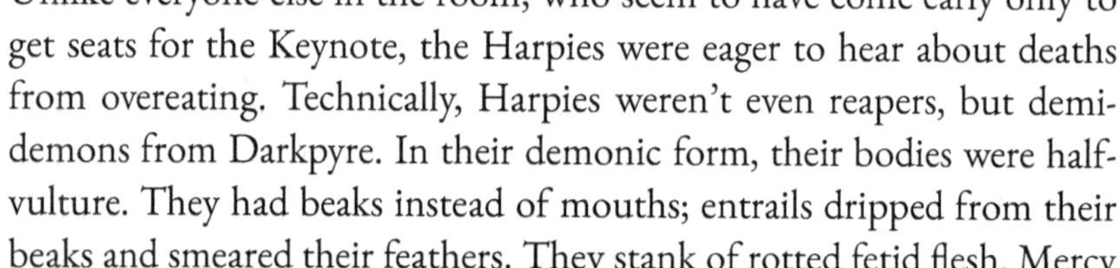

Unlike everyone else in the room, who seem to have come early only to get seats for the Keynote, the Harpies were eager to hear about deaths from overeating. Technically, Harpies weren't even reapers, but demi-demons from Darkpyre. In their demonic form, their bodies were half-vulture. They had beaks instead of mouths; entrails dripped from their beaks and smeared their feathers. They stank of rotted fetid flesh. Mercy did not want to be rude and openly hold her nose, but she wished the Harpies had not stolen seats on her row.

"Not every death I take is the one who overeats," the reaper at the podium pontificated. "Let me tell you about some amazing deaths I got to reap while working in Darkpyre for the Guliks.

"The man we are honored to have as our Keynote Spearker today is not a reaper, but he is an expert on death. King Xin Glug'ulgros of the Guliks—the Demons of Gluttony—literally eats his enemies. Yes—it's true—a little known fact! But logical, if you think about it.

"Being the most powerful Gulik, King Xin Glug'ulgros can acquire the magical power of any creature he eats, so he goes after enemies with powers he wants to acquire. Then he chains them to a spit and starts to roast them and starts eating them while they are still alive. It's really tiresome for me as a reaper, because it takes them so long to die. Every time I think, 'okay, this is it,' the Demon King brings in some minions, usually Fallen Angels, and makes them heal his victim so that the victim's agony will be prolonged. I don't know if he thinks this helps his acquisition of their powers, or if he's just enjoying their agony.

"Anyway, for me as a reaper it means that waiting on the death is usually a many-hour affair! Once I had to stay for thirteen whole days and nights before I finally was able to reap my soul!"

The speaker laughed and the Harpies in the audience all laughed with him. There seem to be more of them now. How many Harpies had come to this conference anyway?

Gross, thought Mercy. No wonder reapers end up with a bad reputation. How could he be laughing about this? Mercy hoped that King Xin Glug'ulgros would talk about solutions to Ghost Overpopulation, as promised in the agenda, and not boast about the enemies he'd devoured.

And where was Miles? How long could it take him to go to the bathroom? The women's bathroom always had long lines at these sorts of events, but she never saw a line at the men's bathroom.

She hoped nothing had gone wrong. She was a little nervous bringing a non-reaper, especially one with his peculiar Hourglass, which she knew would attract unwanted attention from her colleagues. But, as long as he wore the ring she gave him, he should be fine.

Heading back to the main auditorium where the Keynote Address would eventually be held, Miles kept his eyes out for anything unusual. It did seem to him that more heads were turning in his direction. People were looking at him in shock, similar to the expression that the skeleton vendor had given him. But why? Nothing had changed. They hadn't looked at him that way before when he had arrived with Mercy.

As Miles was heading toward the main hall where the keynote speech would be held, he felt a tingling on the hairs at the back of his neck. Alerted that something strange was going on, he followed his instinct, and entered a service area adjacent to the main hall.

He smelled brimstone, the same foul, rotten egg smell that the dark angel created whenever he tore a hole in space to travel. There was no one else in the room, but black smoke billowed out of a rip in the air, and the sulfuric smell intensified. A strange rune or glyph hovered in the air, made out of burning light, similar to some of the symbols he saw sometimes in people's chakras. It acted like the top of a zipper, unraveling existence on either side, exposing something beyond, something unnatural and horrendous.

A gaping wound in reality opened up in front of him.

A huge chamber lay on the other side of that gaping hole. Miles only saw the tableau for a few seconds, but it was frozen in his eidetic memory as if etched in stone.

It was a torture chamber. A familiar figure was bound to a complex contraption that stretched his four limbs and his two huge black wings out like an insect on an etymologist's examination table. It was Raziel Ranaci, worse for the wear. Horned, tailed, blood-red creatures, which Miles instantly knew must be demons, were tormenting the Fallen Angel with various searing, hot prods and knives.

Off to the side of the room was a cage, in which a pig squealed and honked, trying to bite the bars of the cage to gnaw its way free.

At the center of the room, overseeing the torture of the dark angel and the pig, was a huge, bloated demon, as fat as ten of the other ghouls combined. He was more swine-like than the actual pig, but in the exaggerated fashion of a nightmare given fleshy form.

"You brought this on yourself, Fallen Angel," sneered the demon. I told you to get me the codex, and you failed me. I told you to kill the detective, and you lied to me."

The Fallen Angel still had all chakras lit, but they were dimmer than Miles had seen before, as if drained.

The immense, slobbering demon, however, glowed brightly. He *also* had seven radiant chakras. The dark side was more prominent than the light, but he even had those extra two "Yin-Yang" chakras lit up on both sides. How had such a foul creature opened all of his spiritual centers?

"Did you really do that to save the life of that worthless pig?" the demon taunted the angel. "What a fool you are. I will keep this up until you beg me to take his life instead of yours. And it will happen. Everyone breaks eventually. Your pride cannot sustain you much longer."

The demon opened his snout wide. Outwardly, it resembled the snout of a boar, but the multiple rows of teeth looked more like a Great White shark. The demon clamped down on Raziel's arm, biting hard.

The angel screamed. The light in his chakras wavered and dimmed, and the light seemed to flow into the gullet of the demon.

Miles shivered violently. He felt colder than he had on the mountain. What abomination was he witnessing?

The demon pulled back, chewing the piece of flesh he had ripped from Raziel's arm. Black venom drooled from his mouth. The wound oozed with similar foul, black goo, like rancid oil.

The demon leered and gloated briefly over his captives, and then he announced to his prisoners and minions, "And now I shall deliver my speech. But don't worry, the fun will resume when I come back!"

Miles jerked away, hurrying out of the room. He rushed out the door and leaned up against the wall. He could hear the heavy footfalls of the creature as he entered the Mundane Sphere from the hell dimension.

The demon was coming towards the door Miles had just exited.

He didn't want to encounter that creature. Miles rushed broke into an outright sprint. He would rather look like a fool to the other people at the conference than come face-to-face with the master of that torture room.

When he was well away and mingling again with the crowd in the main corridor, only then did Miles start to breathe normally again. His heart was pounding very fast and sweat covered his forehead. He had not been this afraid even when the dark angel had been explaining how he was going to destroy Miles's body so it would not come back to life.

Perhaps Miles had not felt as much fear as he should have. Raziel had been implacable, relentless, and much stronger than Miles, but there had also been an air of sorrow to him, that made it hard to hate him even when he was slapping Miles around with a stick.

The creature from the hell dimension, on the other hand, oozed malice: a fetid, vile, stinking, hatred mixed with a toxic brew of greed and gloating. Up until now, Miles would have said pure evil did not exist. Now, he was not so certain.

Miles recalled what Raziel had said to him. *You will go someplace better. I will go someplace worse...*

Miles felt no joy in seeing the suffering of the dark angel who had tried kill to him, not when it was clear to Miles that the real author of the order was the monster torturing him.

Miles gripped the present he had bought for Mercy. How he longed to take out the scythe and lop off the head of the corpulent demon. He had never had such a burning need to slay another creature as he had now.

But he forced his hands to unclench when he saw he was starting to crinkle the box. He was not a reaper.

He found the row where Mercy awaited him. Some very smelly and obnoxious women had taken up the seats at the edge of the row and he had to pass by them, touching their feathered knees, which terminated in talons, as he passed. He mumbled, "Excuse me... Pardon me, excuse me... So sorry... Just coming right through, sorry about that..."

He reached Mercy at the center of the row.

"What did I miss?" he asked.

"Just a long and gruesome story about the Demon King of Gluttony torturing and eating people to get their powers. It was gross. What took you so long?" She glanced at the box. "You went shopping?"

He had meant to keep it a surprise for later but now he realized that wasn't going to work. Bashfully, he handed it over to her. "It's a present. For you."

"Miles! You didn't have to do that."

"I wanted to. Go on, you might as well open it, I guess."

"It's wrapped so beautifully..." She hesitated. "I hate to tear the paper."

"You can wait if you want."

"Who am I kidding? I can't wait!"

She nonetheless opened the paper in such a way that anyone would've thought she was doing surgery on the seam. She folded it back without ripping it at all. When she peaked inside the box, she immediately recognized the scythe.

Miles watched her face become soft and glowing. Even though Mercy was still in her human form he could see her Valkyrie form shining through, and he could see the unity of her two sides: gentle nurse and fierce warrior. She had never been more beautiful than in that moment and he was glad he had gotten her the present. If this was his reward, he would shower her with presents every day of her life.

She looked up at him and met his eyes. "How did you know...?"

"You stopped at the booth."

"I stopped literally at a hundred booths. How did you know that this is what I wanted more than anything? What kind of magic did you use?"

"Just the magic of close observation, Mercy. I saw how your face lit up when you held the scythe. Just like it did just now when you opened the package. Do you have any idea how beautiful you are?"

Mercy scoffed. "In this form I look like a dumpling, and my other form I'm too severe and scary."

"In this form you look good enough to eat and in your other form you look like you could kick the ass of anyone here. You're beautiful either way."

Her adorable blush climbed all the way from her throat to the tops of her cheekbones.

~

Spontaneously, Mercy tilted her head up to him, leaned close and kissed him softly on the cheek. "Thank you."

He raised his hand to her face and then lowered his lips to hers and kissed her deeply. It was awkward because they were both sitting in the chairs, and the scythe was laying across her lap between them, and yet when his lips met hers and their mouths merged and their tongues touched, her soul glowed, her body tingled, time froze and nothing else mattered.

When they finally broke apart from the kiss, a hush had fallen over the speaker's hall. Mercy blushed again and she realized that their neighbors in the rows in front, to the side, and behind them, were all staring at them. You would think they had never seen anyone kiss in public before. Sure, Mercy could also get annoyed by public displays of affection, but wasn't it even more rude to stare like that?

"Literally everyone is staring at us," she giggled.

He gazed into her face as if he wanted to memorize every feature. "No, they're not," he said. But then, out of habit, he glanced around.

Suddenly he sat up straight and a frown replaced his dreamy expression. "Yes, they are. Why? Don't reapers kiss?"

Mercy also began to grow uneasy. Not only was everyone staring at them, but the reapers were starting to whisper and point. There was an underlying murmur of anger and something else in the voices around them. Ambition. Scheming.

Mercy heard the words, the "Death Evader! Rogue Soul! His Hourglass is upside down!"

Oh. Oh no. She looked at Miles's ring hand and saw that his pointer finger was bare.

"What happened to the ring I gave you?"

"Funny story. I didn't have enough money on my credit card, but the vendor said I could trade the ring... I'm sorry, Mercy, you said it was a gift, so I thought..."

"But you shouldn't have taken it off! It was important! I wouldn't have given it to you if it wasn't important, Miles!"

"If it was important, you should've told me how and why," he said, with a touch of anger. "I thought we agreed we weren't going to keep secrets from each other?"

"I told you before," she hissed. "There's something a little strange about your aura."

The blood drained from his face. The vendor said something about that.

"Strange, how? Why does it matter?" he demanded.

"Because they think you are... They're clearly wrong, but they think you are someone else. Someone that is an enemy of all reapers."

"The enemy of all reapers? Who is that?"

"I don't know who it is. No one does. There's someone supposedly here in Arcana Glen who has been evading death every time it tries to come for him. It's a violation of the law of nature and a personal insult to every reaper. They've probably decided that you could be him because there's something strange about your aura. That's not proof of anything, but some reapers will be willing to try to reap you just in case and let the Light sort it out."

"I hope you're not serious."

"I'm very serious. We better get out of here."

They both stood up.

So did all the reapers seated around them. The Harpies and other non-reapers in the room, were unable to see Miles' strange aura, but they were also aware something was going on.

Meanwhile, an oblivious announcer somewhere chirped happily, "And, now, ladies and gentle-reapers, I am pleased to announce our Keynote Speaker—King Xin Glug'ulgros of the Guliks, Head Devil of Darkpyre, Duke of the Demons of Gluttony, Khan of the Gelatinous Hoards, Tzar of Tartarus, the Overloard of Hell!"

And then the Keynote Speaker waddled onto the stage. It was the corpulent demon who had been torturing and biting Raziel. The demon with all seven chakras that pulsed with stolen light.

At the same moment, Miles recognized him, the Demon King stared straight at Miles and also flinched as if he recognized Miles. Then the demon huffed and puffed up like a thorny, poisonous, puffer fish. The Demon King raised his blubbery arm and pointed at Miles.

"Reap that man and bring his soul to me!"

The Harpies blocking their row leaped up and assumed an aggressive stance. As the mood of the crowd turned into that of a lynch mob, the hoard of reapers and demi-demons moved in on Mercy and Miles.

Twenty-Two

July 23, Saturday

MERCY FLIPPED to her other form. Suddenly, instead of a curvaceous but short young woman with a bob hairdo, she stood seven feet tall, with a crown of wings, a cascade of feathery platinum blonde hair, huge wings of steel and boobs like mountains. Her chain mail bikini clinked and squeaked as she lifted the scythe that Miles had bought her out of it sheath.

"Stand aside from the freak, Mercy!" shouted an unpleasantly familiar voice.

Just great! It was Yorgath the Undying Scourge, her ex.

"This doesn't need to concern you, little girl!" the ugly clown snarled. "We just need to check his soul to see if he's here legitimately!"

"By 'checking' his soul, you mean reap him!" she shouted back.

"That's right!" he smirked. "We can do this the easy way, or the hard way, Mercy. One way or another, he's going down!"

"Like hell he is!" yelled Mercy. "He's here as my guest. He's not who you think he is and nobody is going to reap him. We are walking out of here, and anyone who interferes is going to get the business end of my

162

scythe. You'll have to reap me and send my soul to Darkpyre before I'll let you have him!"

She pulled out her scythe. The sweet hiss of Valhalla-forged steel answered her summons. The scythe was eager to taste blood. Mercy gestured. "Come on, Miles."

In a lower voice, she whispered to him, "Grab onto me, we're going to fly."

He wrapped his arms around her neck. When she was in this form, she was taller than he was. Fortunately, for a guy, he was quite limber. He was muscular as well, no light weight, but in her current form, she hardly felt his weight. She flung wide her steel re-encased wings, kicked over a few chairs, and soared into the air.

Her clown ex attacked first. It was like he felt some lingering jealousy or something. In this form, Mercy felt zero mercy. She swung her scythe and slashed his grinning painted face out of her way. An angry gash striped his white face paint with a red streak. She could have sliced his head off and reaped his soul, but sentiment made her hesitate, and he flew away before she could.

Next, Mercy swiped her scythe at all the flying creatures trying to keep up with her as she soared toward the ceiling. The conference hall of the hotel was taller than a normal room but not a vaulted ceiling or anything she would call spacious. It was a flat ceiling with rectangular lights at regular intervals, and dangerous little sprinkler heads that she knew would leave a scratch if she bumped up against them. She had to fly low and hard with Miles holding on, which slightly threw her off balance.

Meanwhile every winged reaper, floating reaper, demon, and demidemon in the room flew after her. Mercy started laying about with her scythe in a serious manner. She swept this way, swiped that way, somersaulted through the air, and landed a kick on a harpy who got too close. With her scythe she countered deadly attacks with lethal blows of her own, reaping a few reapers souls in the process.

All her battle practice, which she had learned in the fighting dungeons of Valhalla against the greatest warriors of history, came sweeping back into her. All of that fun and games was now put to a deadly purpose. She was serious when she told them that she would rather see her own soul reaped and sent to Darkpyre then allow these creatures to hurt her friend. Miles had been nothing but a gentleman to her and she had no intention of repaying his kindness with betrayal. It was her fault that she had dragged him to a reapers' conference, even knowing full well his strange Hourglass might make him a target.

She wasn't going to let her mistake be paid for with his soul.

Reaper after reaper tried to assault her. They attacked her from the front and behind. Reapers attacked her from all sides at once.

But she had a few tricks of her own. She wove a steel circle of protection with the supernaturally fast motions of her scythe, creating geometrical shapes around her that acted as a magical shield. When she had to focus on the enemy in front of her, her shields created from the light of her scythe lingered like a net of light, preventing enemies from attacking her from behind. Then she had time to turn around and deal with them, as she willed.

Right and left, above and below, to one side and then the other, behind and in front of her, she laid out a path of steel, blood, and destruction that cleared the way from one end of the hallway to the other.

After she had literally slain more than a hundred reapers, the others all fled in terror.

Finally, they landed. They were now outside the hotel.

They were too many humans around for the reapers to risk battling her out here. But Mercy was still buzzing with energy and nervous rage. She felt so upset at what had happened that she could have easily slain another hundred reapers and thought nothing of it.

Then she noticed the expression on Miles's face. He was staring at her as if she were a force of nature, an avalanche, a tsunami, a wildfire, a bolt of lightning striking the earth from out of a clear blue sky. He gaped at her as though he had never seen anything so amazing—or terrifying—in his life.

Her heart sank. Here it came. The moment when the guy she

fancied couldn't put up with the fact that, at her core, she was a terrifying battle goddess.

"Holy moly, Mercy!" Miles shouted. "You are one effing, bad-ass bitch! I love you!"

He threw his arms around her and kissed her. In the midst of the kiss, she melted back down into her tinier, plumper form. She looked up at him with tears in her eyes.

"Are you sure?" she asked. "This is the real me. And that's the real me. They're both me. Can you handle all of me?"

"Give me a lifetime, and then ask me again," he said. "Marry me, Mercy, and make me the happiest man on this 'mundane sphere.'

"I would give you a ring," he added with a twist of his lips. "But I traded mine for the scythe you're carrying. Under the circumstances, it seems like it was probably a timely trade. But I will get you another ring, I promise."

He started to go down on one knee, mumbling, "Oh, I forgot this part..."

She laughed and tugged him back to his feet. "You silly man. Of course, I'll marry you. I love you. You don't think we are moving too fast? We never even met for dinner!"

"You just fought off a whole convention of reapers for me," he said, "I don't want to take any chances that you'll find someone better. I know I never will!"

She laughed and they kissed again. She couldn't believe how quickly her emotions had flipped from rage to ecstasy. This day was just insane.

"I think we still better get as far away from this hotel as we can," she said. "They might regroup and try to attack you again."

"Wait here," he said, "The car is just across the street. You look out for any more reapers, and I'll go get the car."

He jogged across the street. As usual, he was completely aware of his environment, scanning both ways and making sure there was no traffic. Yet when he was halfway across the street a fog suddenly rolled in, a thick, unnatural soup of darkness. A speeding vehicle rolled out of the fog at breakneck speed. It was driven by a reaper... Yorgath the Undying Scourge, her clown ex.

She should have reaped that bastard!

She'd forgotten he had a stallion white Death Car, with the license plate PALHORS. *Gah!* He was such a blowhard.

The white car hit Miles head on and the human man went flying into the air in a way that no human body was ever designed to do. Mercy screamed. She ran up to the body splattered on the pavement, but she already knew it was too late. Her stupid clown ex was laughing his head off in the car, shouting, "I killed him, now I'll reap him!"

Mercy already knew there was nothing she could do to save Miles. No human could survive that. She vented her fury on the laughing clown. She took the scythe Miles had bought her and sliced his head off.

"Not before I reap you, asshole!" She screamed. "Go back to Dark-pyre and hang out with the Harpies!"

～

Miles knew the street was clear when he started to cross it, then out of nowhere, out of fog that had not been there a moment before, he saw a car speeding toward him. He didn't have time to feel the impact. He was vaguely aware of everything spinning upside down.

And then... darkness.

And then... light again.

He opened his eyes and found himself laying on his back, in a pool of sticky mess which he realized was his own blood. His head hurt, his chest hurt, his legs hurt, even his fingers and toes hurt. His everything hurt.

Nonetheless, he dragged himself to his feet, groaning at the pain of bones that felt like they were knitting back together. He touched his skull and brain came away on his fingers, but a moment later, when he rubbed his head again, it was whole and he didn't seem to have missed the extra brain. Well, Miles had always heard that humans only used 10% of their brain. Apparently, that was true. At least of him.

Mercy had beheaded the driver of the car, which was nice of her, he thought. It saved him the trouble of trying to fight the asshole. Anyway, he recognized the driver when he saw the head a few feet away from the car. It was one of the clowns who had attacked him inside the convention hall.

What was with these reapers anyway? Why were they suddenly going after him? Was it just because he was a human at a supernatural convention? But Mercy had said that was allowed. Unusual, not illegal.

Mercy was crying and screaming out his name, apparently heartbroken that he was dead. He was really touched. Miles always secretly feared that he would die one day, maybe run over by a car or stabbed by someone he was investigating and thrown into into a ditch—or hey, dumped in a dumpster—not be discovered for days. He had feared that since his family was gone and his wife had divorced him, that nobody would care whether he lived or died anymore, that no one would even notice his absence. But Mercy was really upset at the thought that she had lost him. More than anything she had said, her grief proved to him that she really did love him.

Better yet, Miles was going to be able to make her very happy by revealing that his injury was not nearly as permanent as she thought.

"Mercy," he said. He didn't tap her shoulder because she was still in her Valkyrie form, and he didn't want her to be startled and accidentally whack off his head when she turned around. "It's okay, I'm here. I'm not dead, I'm alive."

She turned around. Many emotions flooded across her face. At first the shock he expected gave way to the delight he expected. But her emotions didn't end with her throwing her arms around him and kissing him as he had hoped. Instead, the expression on her face continued to evolve into something that resembled horror.

"You came back to life..." she gasped.

"Not really... I mean, I was injured, but I don't think it was as bad as..."

"You were a puddle on the asphalt, Miles! No one could survive that! Not even an arcane could survive that! You came back to life! You defied death! *You really are...* You really are who all the reapers said you were! And I just fought them for you, too! I can't believe I was so stupid! You are the man who refuses to die!"

"Mercy, no... I can explain..." He broke off because, actually, he could *not* explain. Maybe the Magician could explain, but Miles had not signed his stupid non-disclosure agreement to find out what the Magician knew about him that Miles himself did not.

"Okay," Miles amended, "I can't explain right at this moment, but there is probably a good explanation..."

"The explanation is that you are an abomination against nature itself! You are a Rogue Soul!" accused Mercy. "Part of me guessed from the start, but I just couldn't admit it to myself! I'm such a rube! You are an insult to every reaper in existence. And it is my job to reap you!"

Twenty-Three

July 23, Saturday

MERCY RAISED HER SCYTHE. Where the car had failed, she instinctively knew she would be able to sever his soul once and for all from his body.

This was why the spirit of the former Seeress, Sabriel Izbognir, had spoken to Mercy. This was what Mercy should have done from the start. Instead, she had turned on her own kind to protect the enemy of nature itself.

She raised her scythe to strike. Yet tears pricked her eyes and she hesitated. She begged him to understand.

"I'm sorry, Miles. I can't let you keep escaping death. This is my job."

"Are you kidding?" he demanded. "That's what you're going to go with? *It's not personal, it's business?'* While you're at it, why not just add, '*It's not you, it's me.'* How about, '*I just need a little time to figure out who I am alone, before I know who I can be with someone else.'* How about..."

A shot rang out behind him.

A red rose bloomed on his chest, visible even in the stains of darker blood that had already turned his white shirt brown. His body tumbled to the pavement once again, and behind him, Mercy saw Sumiko the Shinigami standing there with a smoking gun.

"I'm sorry, Mercy," said Sumiko. "I could tell you didn't really want to do it, but it had to be done."

But as Mercy looked down at Miles, she could see his Hourglass lying on its side. Like an infinity sign. And very, very slowly, it was still ticking like a clock that had not yet run out. That was when she realized that she truly was *the only one* who could kill him. She didn't know why. And she also didn't know if she could bring herself to do it. She should've said something to Sumiko, but instead Mercy only nodded her head once, as if accepting the inevitable.

Deep inside, her emotions were in turmoil. She had not made any decision at all. She had not yet accepted anything. She had always told those she reaped that they should fight death to the very end. Wasn't that what Miles was doing?

Sumiko and Mercy both heard the siren at the same time.

"The humans are sending an ambulance," said Sumiko. "They'll take him to the hospital. Mercy, you have to make sure he doesn't come back again."

"I'll go with him," whispered Mercy. "I'll make sure."

Sumiko nodded, accepting this promise at face value.

But Mercy asked herself, *You'll make sure of what?* That he accepted death finally? Or would she make sure that he was able to escape once again?

No matter what she did, she knew they could not be together. If he escaped death, he would be on the run for the rest of his life, always one step ahead of the reapers sent after him to collect on his debt to the universe. There was no way she would be able to go with him. She would only draw attention to him. Besides, she would have to face the judgment of her own people for having fought them tooth and nail to defend a mortal who refused to die.

～

Mercy was not surprised they took him to her own hospital, the Veteran's Hospital. It was the closest hospital with an emergency room. Otherwise, they would've had to drive him down the mountain to a bigger town with better facilities.

All three doctors were on duty over the weekend. That was unusual. She knew that Dr Cornel was on duty, but she had not expected to see Dr Winters there. She wasn't certain about Dr Sharpe's schedule, but he was the one on duty in the emergency room when they arrived there.

By the time they rushed Miles to emergency surgery, however, there was little to be done. And not, as one might think, because he died *en route*, as one would normally expect of a human shot directly through the heart. Rather, by the time Miles was rolled on a gurney into the operating room, he was already whole again.

Dr Sharpe declared that the bullet must have missed his body completely.

"Couldn't the idiots in the ambulance have saved me the trouble by figuring this out for themselves?" ranted the doctor.

Mercy peeked over Dr Sharpe's shoulder. Sure enough, there was no bullet and no bullet hole in the smooth chest of the man on the operating table. The only reason he remained unconscious is that he had been given drugs.

Amazing, thought Mercy. A bullet couldn't stop him. Being hit by a car couldn't stop him. But anesthesia could knock him out just like any other man.

Dr Sharpe forced her to leave the emergency room. Dazed, she obeyed, reporting in to the nursing station by rote. Miles would survive —which meant she had to kill him.

What would she do?

Miles kept his eyes closed after he regained consciousness. He didn't want to be killed again as soon as he sat up. He listened carefully, trying to determine if he was still in the emergency room surrounded by angry reapers.

From the sounds, he concluded, nope, not in the street. In a hospital, surrounded by anxious doctors. That would have been better, except he knew that at least one, possibly all three of the doctors at this hospital were murderers, using magic to steal the souls of healthy men to revive dying men were infiltrated into the military base. Every single one went on to join the same unity, which Maverick deemed highly significant, something to do with "KADABRA."

Who was pulling the strings? Surely not the murdering doctors, they were only the intermediaries.

Miles opened his eyes just a crack. Dr Sharpe had his back to him. He was the only one in the room with Miles. For some reason, Dr Sharpe had sent the nurses away.

Dr Cornel rushed into the room, holding a ruby, red jewel. "Don't give up yet!" cried Cornel. "I have a way to save him..."

Dr Sharpe looked up at the other doctor in disgust. "I thought you must have already used one of your toys on him. He was supposedly shot, but nothing's wrong with him."

Cornel paused, confused. "I didn't."

"Warren must have used the jewel on the patient, then," concluded Sharpe.

"But Dr Winters never uses the jewels," said Cornel, looking puzzled.

"You're so naive, Augustus," sneered Sharpe. "Warren uses those even more than you do. But unlike you, he's subtle about it and doesn't seek credit. Probably because he knows that if it ever got out how those things really work, he'd be sent to prison. So he slips you a few, so if he gets caught, he'll use you as a scapegoat."

"But why would anyone object to saving lives?" asked Cornel. "That's our job!"

"Because these jewels obey the rules of Dark magic, not mundane physics," declared Dr Warren Winters as he swept into the room. "And Dark magic always demands a sacrifice."

Dr Augustus Cornel's mouth flapped but no words came out. He was speechless with shock.

"Allow me to demonstrate," said Dr Winters smoothly. In a single, ruthless motion, he thrust the pointy tip of a clear jewel into Dr Cornel's heart.

Miles tried to get up, to stop the murder, but his body wasn't ready to move yet. He was still mostly dead.

Cornel gasped; his eyes rolled back in his head; his face turned blue. He sagged to the ground.

Winters kicked the body. "Cardiac arrest. How tragic. Such a promising young doctor, don't you agree, Dick? You shouldn't have blabbed to him. You cost him his life."

Dr Sharpe backed away from Dr Winters in terror. "Warren... please... I didn't really know... I only suspected... I won't say anything... please..."

Warren Winters pulled out a gun with his left hand and shot Sharpe twice, once in the lung and once in the kidney.

"You're dying quickly from exsanguination and pneumothorax," diagnosed Warren Winters with an unpleasant smile. "Or do you want to live?"

He held up the jewel, which, after being used to steal Cornel's life-force, glowed deep, ruby red.

"...please... save me..." wheezed Sharpe.

Dr Winters placed the blood red jewel over Sharpe's heart. This time, instead of hurting him, as the gem drained of color, Sharpe's wounds closed, and he recovered.

"Now you won't tell anyone," said Dr Winters. "Because if you do, it will come out that you traded Cornel's life to save your own. You're implicated, Dick. And your soul now belongs to my master."

"W...who is your m... master?" stammered Sharpe.

Winters smiled. "You'll serve him at the end of your borrowed life."

Mercy was off duty, but no one questioned the fact that she wanted to visit a patient. Since Miles was unconscious, although apparently healthy, he was taken to a regular room to wake up and sign out and Mercy joined him there. Even those who didn't know that she and Miles were dating were used to her spending time with patients whether she was on call or not.

She stood by his bedside watching him rest. He looked peaceful and handsome and perfectly adorable when he slept. She wanted to stroke his hair from his face and caress his cheek. She wanted to gently kiss his lips and see if she could wake him up like Princess Beauty with Sleeping Charming.

What she was supposed to do was chop off his head the way she had done with her ugly clown ex.

A Door appeared at the foot of the hospital bed. It looked like an ordinary door in an ordinary human building with a door handle of shiny brass and white paint, but Mercy immediately recognized it as a door to one of the other Spheres. The Door opened and she half expected to see either one of her parents, or her ex, or all of them together, pour through and start yelling at her for her completely messing up everything about being a reaper.

Instead, it was the spirit of Sabriel who came through. Her features looked different, since now she wasn't wearing another person's body. The "real" Sabriel had the same coloring as Kyrah: pale skin, dark hair, purple eyes, and coral lips. But that was not how Mercy recognized her. She could sense the energy from the spirit. Of course, being a spirit, there was no Hourglass superimposed over Sabriel. She was here only as a visitor, like a ghost, but not here against her will.

"You came all the way from the Last Home?" asked Mercy in amazement. It was one thing for a spirit to speak through a physical body during a seance, as Sabriel had done earlier through Kyrah. It was another for the spirit to come of its own accord to the Mundane Sphere.

"This is important," said Sabriel. "He is unconscious now and defenseless. You can reap him, and he won't be able to fight you. Quickly, do it now! Take his soul and send him through this Door!"

"I will," said Mercy. And yet she did not draw her scythe. "But can you tell me where he will go after...?"

"That is not for me to decide," said Sabriel. She looked anxiously at the man in the hospital bed. "Mercy, you must hurry! He is starting to wake up."

"Really? The anesthetic should've kept him out for hours. I guess whatever magic he has to evade death also does work somewhere on the drugs…"

"Do it now!" commanded Sabriel , growing impatient.

"Miles, wake up!" said Mercy. "Wake up Miles!"

"What are you doing!" cried Sabriel.

"If I'm going to reap the man I love," Mercy said severely, "I'm going to do it when he is awake. I'm not going to murder him in his sleep!"

~

Miles realized there was no point any longer in pretending to be asleep. He opened his eyes.

He looked directly at Mercy. "I am awake."

He sat up. He noted Sabriel hovering near a floating door. He recognized her from the file the Magician had shown him—she was one of the dead Guardians. What was she doing here?

Instead of asking Mercy directly, Miles made a show of being exasperated at his attire. "A hospital gown? Really? Can I at least die in something a little more dignified? I don't suppose you have a change of clothes around here for a guy my size."

"Actually," said Mercy, "because we have a lot of Shifters at this hospital, we do keep changes of clothes in the closet."

The hovering spirit of Sabriel looked annoyed that he ignored her. Apparently, even the ghosts of Guardians hated being ignored by the living.

Mercy went to the closet and fetched him clothes. He dressed himself and she turned her back to give him privacy.

"What are you doing?" reproached the spirit of Sabriel. "Why aren't you slaying the man who refuses to die? Slay him before he attacks you!"

"Are you going to attack me, Miles?" asked Mercy.

"No," he said. "Not that I would have much chance against a Valkyrie if I did."

"Do you understand why I have to reap you?"

Miles nodded his head. He couldn't deny it any longer. "I kept telling myself that I wasn't really dying and coming back to life," he said.

"I wasn't trying to deceive you, Mercy. I was trying to deceive myself. But I can't deny it any longer. For some reason, Death just doesn't seem to want to take me."

"About a hundred dead reapers and hundreds more who would be dead except they're cowards would say otherwise," sneered Sabriel. The spirit of the beautiful woman still hovered near the Door.

"Yeah, well it's not that I have been trying to evade death, in the way you keep describing it," said Miles. "In fact, if anything, most people would tell me that lately I've been courting death." He winked at Mercy and she giggled, although her laughter turned into a gasp of sadness.

He faced her. "But, hey… If what's been going on with me is unnatural and upsetting some kind of necessary balance in the cosmos, then I'm willing to take my licks. Do what you have to do, Mercy. I just want you to know before you swing that scythe, that even though you're going to kill me with it, I am glad I bought it for you. I love you."

"Oh vomit," said Sabriel in the background. "Can you please stop?"

Normally, Miles would've been the one feeling nauseated by the mushy love talk. But now he finally understood what was so fantastic about whispering sweet nothings. Somehow, the fact it made the haughty spirit miserable only made him happier. He moved in and kissed Mercy soundly on the lips. First, he did it just to piss off the spirit, but then he got lost in the kiss and was glad he did it. Finally, he stepped backwards and bared his neck like a prisoner on his way to a beheading.

"Go ahead," he said. "Just slice me open. I hope it will stick this time. I really have no control over it."

"If *she* does it, it will work," promised Sabriel.

Mercy lifted her scythe and once again her arms felt like lead. She could not do it.

"I just can't."

The spirit drifted closer to Mercy with a greedy expression on her face. "Let me into your body. Let me control your scythe and your arms. I will help you do it."

The spirit went so far as to start to slither into the Mercy's body.

Miles opened his eyes very wide. When Sabriel entered the body of Mercy, for a moment, *all* of her chakras lit up.

Mercy pushed the spirit physically out of her body and spirit stumbled back.

"Do I look like a medium to you?" demanded Mercy. "What part of Valkyrie do you not understand? I don't need some ghost telling me how to do my job!"

"Then do your job!" snapped Sabriel.

"Wait!" cried Miles. "Mercy, I need you to hold off on reaping me until I finish one thing. You've got to trust me on this. You can reap me, eventually, and restore the cosmic balance. Just give me a chance to report my findings to the Magician first. I think I've solved one case, and I have relevant information for the other case."

"What is he talking about?" demanded Sabriel. "What business do you have with the Magician, Rogue Soul?"

He had noticed a sign glow on the Door at the same moment that Sabriel had tried to possess Mercy's body. The symbol was like the chemical symbols he saw superimposed in the chakras when he looked at people. He traced the sigil that was there – it was only glowing letters and lights—and created his own symbol by drawing it with his finger. As he expected, his finger was able to leave a glowing residue on the spirit Door.

"Do you have to kill me to take me through THIS door?"

"She doesn't control what door you go through, you idiot," said the spirit of Sabriel.

"She's right," said Mercy. "I have no control over it. I'm sorry."

"Mercy, I've seen what you can do. And I've seen how everyone is depending on you to kill me for some reason. No other reaper can do it. Your cute little Japanese friend tried, and she failed. Your less cute friend with the clown face tried, and he failed too. You know and I know there's only really one reason that you are able to do it and no one else. You must be what these people have been looking for, the Guardian of Death. And that means you can open any Door you want including this one."

"But I don't know where this Door goes," protested Mercy.

Miles smiled. "But I do."

"Miles, I can only take you through if you're dead."

"Then kill me. If that's what it takes."

Mercy started to shake her head, but he said impatiently, "You have to do it."

Sabriel said, "For once, I agree with the monster who defies nature. You have to do it—kill him and reap him! It doesn't matter what Door, you take him through as long as he doesn't stay here."

"Fine!" cried Mercy. And she sliced Miles through with her scythe.

Twenty-Four

July 23, Midnight on Saturday

MERCY KILLED Miles a third time in an hour, but she didn't stop there. She could already see that his soul wasn't going anywhere. Most souls were expelled when unbearable pain ripped through the body. The soul inside Miles responded differently. His soul seemed to treat death as simply another injury, a mild injury, something to be suffered through and endured, like standing upside down on one's head for a while, before returning to the normal upright position.

But this time, Mercy reached her hand past his flesh and grabbed his spirit directly. Then she flew with his spirit through the Door.

They traveled through the Void between the Spheres. Miles looked around as curiously as he had when he had been at the reapers' convention. Of course, in the void there was nothing to see, no sound to hear, no smells to smell, nothing to touch. It was just pure emptiness. The sense of travel was conveyed by one's own body moving, but even that was only an illusion.

Sabriel traveled with them for a little while. But soon her bright white spirit parted ways with theirs and disappeared toward another destination. The Door that they were flying through opened up, showing a new place.

When Mercy saw where they headed, she gasped in horror. "No, no, this can't be right! We don't want to go there, Miles! That's Darkpyre—the place that you humans call Hell!"

"That's exactly where I want to go," said Miles. "And you are the only way I can get there."

~

They arrived in a huge Hall, something more elaborate and ostentatious than even the grand lobby of the casino back in Arcana Glen. In fact, all earthly architecture was put to shame by the glitz and glam of this hallway, and yet there was something unpleasant about it. The air was rancid and heavy, the gravity felt too strong, depression weighed upon the soul as soon as one entered, and everything felt harder and bleaker and crueler and meaner.

There was great display of wealth and abundance here and yet no satisfaction or satiation to be found. Seven Kings sat up at a table, arrayed like lords at a medieval table in a feudal castle. Down the length of the hall, longer tables ran, at which were seated the demon lords and princes. The tables were piled with food of all sorts. The demons were drinking and laughing and carousing as if they were having great fun, although all of them wore expressions of deep misery and paranoia.

Just as in a medieval banquet, hunting Hellhounds were chasing something in the center of the room, causing great amusement to all the demons. The Hellhounds—huge, smoking, black hounds with burning red eyes—were chasing a horned swine, a fat, pink and black pig. The swine was fighting them, but the hounds outnumbered it. The demons were laughing uproariously at this as if they were in on some inside joke that Miles could not understand. They were also taking bets on how long it would take the hounds to tear this swine apart.

Miles and Mercy flew through the Door and landed in the chamber. Fortunately for them, they came from a side door near the back, so they were not visible to the Demon Kings who faced forward.

Miles peered around the chamber and finally perceived what the demons were laughing about along with the swine and the wolves.

Raziel had been strung upside down between a crossbeam set on two wooden pillars. He had been tied by one foot. His other foot dangled. His only clothing was a rag, torn and ripped.

A demon stood behind Raziel, whipping him. Another demon stood in front of him with a fiery brand, touching it to his body to make him scream. His formally glorious sleek, burning black wings were tattered and broken.

Beside him, Mercy gasped softly.

"He's an angel," she hissed. Outrage filled her voice. If she hadn't already been in her Valkyrie form, she would have switched to it, he was sure. "They are torturing an angel!"

"Shhh," hushed Miles. "If we draw attention to ourselves, I don't think will ever leave this place."

"Why are we even here? We don't belong here," she said. "I can tell this is not where you belong, so why did you make me bring you here?"

"I am here on business for the Magician," he said. "And I need you to take me back once we're done. After that, you can reap me for real. Let me finish my job first, okay? I've never done a half-assed job before, and I don't want to start now. You stay here. I'm going to get a better look at the demons. If they catch me, save yourself—don't try to save me."

He crept against the wall, trying to get into a position where he could see everyone in the room without being seen.

Miles had been afraid that his ability to see chakras would not work in another Sphere. Hell, he'd been afraid that he wouldn't be able to travel to a literal hell at all. Only now that he physically saw it, so to speak, did he really believe that it really existed. His power to see chakras did extend to demons; he could see all of them, including the one demon who had seven activated chakras.

The only non-demon sitting at the table with the Kings had his back to Miles. And Miles recognized that back. This was the same man who had been taking to Dr Warren Winters.

This man also had seven activated chakras, including the two doubled chakras which indicated he had nine forms of magic, dark and light.

The guest was apparently another king, for he wore a crown of clear crystal that looked like the same material the "miracle" jewels were made of. He wore a pale blue robe, a rich garment embroidered with alchemical symbols—and snowflakes. His hair was snow white and his skin pale as bleached bones. When he turned slightly, Miles saw his pointed ears.

Miles had seen enough. He floated back toward Mercy, eager to get away before the hordes of hell discovered a wayward, vulnerable spirit in their midst.

Mercy had no intention of remaining idle while the demons were torturing an angel. As long as she was here, she could do something useful and rescue that poor being. He had been so badly abused that his halo no longer glimmered around his body. His Hourglass indicated that his lifeforce had drained almost to the end, with only a sliver of sand left in the top, rapidly falling toward the huge pile at the bottom.

However, even as Mercy watched, a Harpy flew down from the rafters where a number of them were perched. The vulture-winged woman stuck her beak into the angels mouth and regurgitated some kind of substance. If it tasted as bad as it smelled, it must have been foul. The angel resisted the vomit. But the crude substance must have also had some rough healing properties, because after the Harpy force-fed the angel, his lifeforce looked reversed in his Hourglass. He now had more sand in the top cup and the grains of life fell less quickly toward the pile in the bottom of the Hourglass.

"You won't escape us that quickly, Seraph!" bellowed Glug'ulgros the Demon King who reigned at the head of the feast. Mercy stared. The Keynote Speaker! He was an enormous fat fellow with a pig nose and pig ears, the usual demon horns, and tusks like a wild boar. "Your use as a source of information may have dried up, but your use as a source of entertainment and energy snacks will last us many, many years to come. You will long for the kiss of a reaper, but no reaper will dare come to you here, not as long as we hold you in our grasp!"

"Think again, you pig!" shouted Mercy. She flew straight at the angel and slashed the cord binding his foot with one swipe of her scythe. Not even demon chains, steeped in Dark magic, could withstand the slice of a reaper's scythe. In a swift motion, she swooped the tortured angel into her muscular Valkyrie arms and threw him over her shoulder before he could hit the floor. His wings were nothing but bloody tatters. There was no way he could fly on his own, but in her Valkyrie form she was strong enough to carry him.

"Miles, we have to go!" Mercy shouted. Although Miles was here like a ghost, in spirit form, if he didn't leave with her, she feared he would be trapped here and reincarnated as a low-level fiend in the Slave Pits near the Lake of Darkfire.

The enraged demons had not noticed Miles yet, but they definitely noticed Mercy. The Seven Kings started hurling huge spells of powerful and demonic magic at her. The Harpies on the rafters dive-bombed her, screeching and hissing.

But suddenly, from behind them all, Miles came leaping like an acrobat. He kicked food in their faces from the table. Even as a ghost, he was the most powerful kind, a poltergeist. He punched a Harpy who tried to grab him, kicked a few more, and then held up his arms for Mercy to grab his hand.

She opened the Door and was about to fly through, when the angel struggled in her arms.

"Get the pig, get the pig!" he rasped. "He's a person under a curse, not an animal!"

Mercy scooped down in the air, like a Ferris Wheel spinning, low enough for the angel to grab the pig in his arms.

Then all of them—Valkyrie, Angel, Miles as a ghost, and the Cursed Swine—all flew through the Door while behind them an army of demons raged and spat futile curses.

~

July 24, just past midnight, early Sunday

They emerged from a Door that opened right back in the hospital room they had left. Miles checked the clock. He had heard that time operated in different Spheres in different ways, but as far as he could tell, they had spent the exact same amount of time in Darkpyre as had passed back here on earth.

Miles drifted over to his body and settled into it. He woke up feeling refreshed. In fact, he felt a lot better than he had as a spirit in Darkpyre There was something about that place that was awful beyond any reasonable explanation based on the physical appearance alone. As rich and indulgent as the chamber and the feast had looked, there had been something deeply unnerving about it, a darkness that weighed on the soul.

Mercy set the pig on the floor and the angel in a hospital bed. She transformed back in her human form.

The angel still looked horrid, but he seemed to gain strength now that he was away from the poisonous atmosphere of Darkpyre. The wild boar ran around the room knocking things over and generally causing trouble with its tusks and it's noisy squealing. With a sigh, the angel pulled himself to his feet.

"You should rest," Mercy told him.

He glanced at her, his bruised face inscrutable. He whistled to the pig, which ran to him. He stumbled out of bed, picked up the swine, and held it tightly. As heavy as the beast was, and although he himself was still injured from the torture he had endured, the angel lifted the pig as though the pain didn't matter.

Miles wondered if what the angel had said to Mercy was correct. Was the animal truly a person who has been transformed into a pig? Miles guessed that, if magic was real, a curse that transformed a man into a pig was a thing that could happen. Who knew?

"You should not have saved me," the angel said harshly to Mercy. "I am not on your side."

He carried the pig out of the room and hurried away down the hall of the hosipital.

"What the hell was that supposed to mean?" asked Miles.

"That's a mystery to me. Just like it's a mystery to me why we went there. And what am I going to do with you? I know you're not on my side either. So why do I feel like you are?"

"I certainly have no wish to be your enemy," said Miles. "As I said back in hell, or Darkpyre, or whatever you call it, all I want is to be able to finish the job that the Magician paid me to do. You know how important it is. *You* knew before I ever even heard of it. I have gathered important information for him. Once I've given that to him, you can take me through another Door. Hopefully not back *there*, unless I've earned it."

He looked glum but determined.

Mercy shook her head vigorously. "I told you that you have not. I think that since you are a fighter, you should come to Valhalla. But I don't know if I will be able to take you there."

"I'm going summon the Magician now," said Miles.

"Do you have a spell to do that?"

He pulled out a cell phone.

Twenty-Five

July 24, past midnight, early Sunday

MILES WAS ONLY JOKING about magically summoning the Magician, but as soon as he called, the Magician responded exactly as if a spell has been cast. He appeared out of thin air, right there in the hospital room. He wasn't alone.

The three people that they had met at the reapers' convention were there as well. Kyrah the Seeress, the blond girl called Bethany, and the golden angel in gold armor, Michael.

"It's about time that you reported in…" The Magician began to say.

Suddenly a pig ran through the door and straight at the blond girl.

The angel was hot on his heels. "You stupid pig, we can't be here when they come… Oh nuts." He skidded to a halt having caught sight of the three Guardians.

"Raziel!" Wrath filled Michael's face. "You! You traitor!"

The Magician raised a Wand and pointed it at Raziel.

The pig bumped into Bethany, who tripped and squealed and toppled into the Magician, throwing off his aim.

The pig having, rubbed itself against Bethany's bare leg, suddenly transformed into a stark-naked man.

The naked man ran back towards Raziel, grabbed the injured angel, and then snapped his fingers to create a puff of vile stinking smoke. Both of them vanished from the hospital room.

"What in the name of the Light is going on in here!" shouted Michael.

"That pig just touched me and turned into a demon named Vass," said Bethany. "And then Vass used his demon snappy power to transport himself and Raziel out of here."

"I know that," said Michael, "But why were they here?"

He glared at Mercy, but Miles answered him.

"We took a little visit to Darkpyre, and we picked up some hitch-hikers along the way," said Miles. "But they aren't really what's important right now. What's important, Magician, is that I have your list of suspects."

"Wait," said Kyrah, gesturing to Miles but speaking to the other Guardians, "Isn't this the man that all the reapers were trying to apprehend? And isn't this the Valkyrie who turned against her own people to defend him?"

"I can explain that," began Miles. "None of it is her fault..."

"It's all my fault," began Mercy.

"Fault?" asked the Magician. "What fault? You did what needed to be done. You culled the ranks of excess reapers. You were the strongest in battle, which means that you are the new Guardian of Death."

"But I thought you had another way to find..." Mercy began.

"I had hoped so too," said Kyrah with a sigh. "But apparently not. I have already asked the other reapers what they want to do with you, and they want you to speak tomorrow, on the final day of their convention. They are very excited to have found the head of their order at last."

"I hate to tell you this," whispered Miles to Mercy, "But you have one seriously messed up profession."

"Nursing *is* ruthless," said Mercy. "Oh... Were you talking about being a reaper?"

"Alephander," Michael said. Michael still looked miffed. "Am I to understand that the man you hired to investigate the Massacre of the Guardians is actually the same man who refuses to die, the one who provoked all the reapers at the convention into a rage?"

"That's right," said Alephander, perfectly calm.

"But then don't we have to let the reapers have him?"

"After I give my report," said Miles. "If everyone could please stop interrupting me so I can finish my job."

"You haven't even started your job yet," said Alephander. "And no one is going to reap you for a long time to come. Your job, if you would have ever bothered to sign the NDA, is to be a Guardian. The Guardian of the Hanged. Sometimes it is also known as the *Path of Sacrifice* or *New Perspectives*. I've known who you really were for a long time, and you would've known it a long time ago as well, if you had not been such a stubborn..."

"Wow, you mean we're both new Guardians?" grinned Miles. "That's pretty cool. How many Guardians are there? How many were you trying to find replacements for?"

The Magician glared at him.

"Dumb question," said Miles. "Twenty-one were killed, so I bet you need replacements for... Can I deliver my report now?"

"Please." Alephander looked as exasperated it as Miles felt, although not nearly as confused. "But we aren't going to do it here. Let us go someplace more comfortable."

The Magician snapped his fingers, just as Raziel had done. But instead of foul-smelling smoke, everyone in the room disappeared from the hospital and reappeared somewhere else. This time they were in a beautiful library with a view of the mountains. Miles recognized it as the library in the Magician' Castle.

～

July 24, Sunday Afternoon

It transpired that many other interruptions prevented Miles from giving his report until later that afternoon.

First, he and Mercy had to prove, formally, that they were Guardians by entering the Temple of the Guardians together. They had to enter a tunnel of light...

Through a safe.

Bizarre, Miles thought. There was no accounting for the tastes of Wizards.

Mercy and Miles walked hand-in-hand into the Temple with the other Guardians. Then the other Guardians bowed to them and called them "*Sarmati*," and "*Sarmat*," and that was that.

Miles sat down in his "throne" and fell asleep. Mercy yelled at the other Guardians that he was exhausted, and still mostly dead, and even the Hanged Man needed time to recover from three deaths in a row within twenty-four hours.

Miles roused himself long enough to stumble into a guest room and fall asleep again.

When he awakened again, the Guardians had already had lunch, but fresh food was served to Miles by ghosts. The ghosts were friendly with Miles, but they swerved around Mercy, darting nervous looks at her. They also avoided the blonde woman, Bethany Guiscard, for some reason.

Miles realized he still had a lot to learn about being a wizard.

"If I had known I was going to be recruited to be the Hanged Man, I would gone to wizard school," Miles apologized as he joined the other Guardians at a large banquet table. "But, with my attitude, I probably would have been *ex-spelled*. Are there any other famous wizard detectives? I would love to meet *Warlock Holmes*."

Groans and threats of death ensued.

"Is he always like this?" asked a sexy woman with cat ears.

"Only when he's breathing," said Mercy. She turned to Michael, a Guardian whose title was The Hierophant. He was an angel, though his wings burned with white and gold light.

"You recognized the angel we rescued from Darkpyre."

"Raziel was once my friend," said Michael sadly. "My best friend since childhood. I don't know what happened to him, why he turned his back on the Light. A while back, he threw his lot in with the demons. We don't know exactly when he turned. You can see how they repaid him."

"Was I wrong to rescue him?" asked Mercy. "I just couldn't stand to see him tormented and humiliated. I know he tried to kill Miles—"

"He didn't try, he succeeded," corrected Chet. "He failed only because the Hanged Man can only be killed by Death herself."

Mercy looked up, surprised. "But I did kill him. I took him to Darkpyre."

Michael waved his hand. "You weren't officially the Guardian of Death yet. You were Called; you had the Power; but you had not yet Presented yourself with your Beloved at the Temple. After the Massacre, the dying Guardian of Love cast a spell requiring all new Guardians to demonstrate their commitment by entering the Temple together. You became Death when you and Miles took your Thrones at the Round Table of Guardians."

"Oh." Mercy paused. "Fine. But about Raziel—I know he killed Miles—"

"Twice, technically," Miles piped up.

"—but nobody deserves to be treated like that!" finished Mercy.

"You were named Mercy for a reason," said Michael. "Never be ashamed of granting mercy, even to those who haven't earned it."

"What about the pig?" asked Miles. "He was mighty attached to that pig."

"That was Vassily Glug'ulgros, son of Xin Glug'ulgros." Another Guardian, who looked suspiciously to Miles like a demon himself, cleared his throat. "Nice to meet you, Miles. I'm Chet. Before I switched sides, I worked with Vass. He *was* a prince in hell, before his transformation, and, his, ah, demotion by his father."

"Ah, yes, the porculent King of Hell," said Miles. "What a swell guy. Sure knows how to throw a party. That brings me to the report."

Miles glanced around the dining table. Thirteen people sat around a table designed to seat twice that number, but Alephander Guiscard was missing. "Where is the Magician?"

And just like that, Alephander Guiscard popped into thin air, appearing at the far end of the table. He seated himself and steepled his fingers.

"Proceed, detective."

"I had two cases to solve," said Miles. "They turned out to be intertwined. One case was the murder of a young, healthy soldier named Gawain Herle. But he was just one of many soldiers dying before their time at the Veteran's Hospital. I uncovered a scheme by an Azir... uh, the Azir *are* the Winter Elves, right?"

The others nodded.

"Right, an Azir named Warren Winters... wow, he didn't really pick a clever alias, did he? How did anyone think he was a Spring Elf with a name like that? Anyway, Winters was running a scam where he used Dark magic devices made with Elemental Wind magic to steal lifeforce from the healthy to revive the dying. The dying soldiers who accepted the help sold their souls to our friend the Demon King... I can't pronounce his name, so I'll just call him Glug. Glug then had an army of agents to infiltrate the military base. Mr Cade," Miles tipped an imaginary hat to the Robot Guardian, Maverick Cade, "was able to hack the base's records and determine that this has been going on for well over a decade.

"Winters earned a lot of money, and he tricked the other, human doctors into looking the other way by bribing them with access to the 'miracle' technology."

A Guardian with the grandiose title of Emperor, an incongruously boy-next-door fellow, interjected, "Victoria and I have apprehended Winters and Cornell. They will face justice in the arcane courts."

"How does this relate to the Massacre of the Guardians?" continued Miles. "I don't know for certain that it does, but I was asked to identify who had enough magic to be able to design the massive nine-magics spell that induced all the Guardians to annihilate each other.

"I identified five suspects. One, is Glug himself."

"No demon has all nine forms of magic," objected Chet. "A demon can't generate Light magic, for one thing. And Elemental magic is not our forte either. We excel in mental forms of magic, and, of course, Dark magic."

"Glug has apparently been able to augment his inborn skills by devouring the powers of his enemies," said Miles. He cringed, remembering the dungeon tableau he had witnessed. "I saw him take a bite of Raziel and feed on his light. It was..." Miles gagged. "The point is, Glug may have cheated, but he has all nine forms of magic now. He's a suspect."

"Interesting," said the Magician. "I suspected him for a long time, but had to dismiss him because I thought he lacked the capacity. This is helpful. Go on."

"The next suspect is the former Seeress, Sabriel," said Miles.

"She's not a suspect!" Alephander said instantly.

Miles looked at him in surprise. Had the unflappable Alephander Guiscard actually expressed an impulsive emotion?

The other Guardians all concurred.

"She's dead," said cat-ears. What was her name? Moxie, the Guardian of Strength. "You know that, right?"

"She died in the Massacre itself!" several other Guardians rushed to point out.

"But she possessed Kyrah, and she tried to possess Mercy," said Miles. "Maybe she acted like a suicide-bomber, killing herself along with others, but knowing she'd be able to come back as a spirit and possess a body."

"It's not that simple, Hanged One," said Kyrah, the current Seeress. "Not even the most powerful spirit can possess a body for long without killing the host."

"She tried to trick Mercy into killing me," Miles pointed out.

"The last Hanged Man turned evil and made an alliance with the demons," said Kyrah. "Sabriel probably feared you would do the same. She may have even confused you with him. Spirits can't always tell the present from the past."

"When Sabriel tried to possess Marcy, I also perceived that Sabriel has all seven chakras open to the nine forms of magic," said Miles.

"Everyone already knew that, but Sabriel couldn't have done it," said Alephander flatly. "Move on. You said you had three other suspects."

"The third suspect was also involved in the scheme to siphon corrupted souls from the Veteran's Hospital to the military base," said Miles. "I was able to finally see his face when Marcy took me to Dark-pyre. He was there, dining with the demons. I recognized him from the report on Sabriel Izbognir. I believe his name is Belleqas Izbognir, her former husband, the King of Swords."

A grim muttering went round the table. This one didn't surprise anyone.

"The King of the Azir has long been a suspect," said Alephander. "But, again, suspicion and proof are two different things. You were able to confirm that he has all nine forms of magic?"

"Yes. Absolutely. Clear as the sun at noon."

"And the fourth suspect?"

"I don't have a name. Another woman. Dumpy, middle aged. Forgettable face. But brilliant magic, all seven chakras, the most perfect balance of light and dark of any that I've seen. All the others leaned this way or that; their magic was full, but a little lumpy, if you know what I mean.

"Not this woman. She had the whole kit'n'kaboodle, yet everything shone in perfect equipoise. Like a chakra diagram given living form. Just... beautiful."

"You're starting to make me jealous," said Mercy.

"Sorry, sweetheart. You know your chakras are my favorite."

"Where did you see her?" asked Alephander.

"Main Street. Just walking along, like anyone. Then she turned into a store with no back door... and vanished."

The Guardians tried to guess who the fourth woman was.

"Someone with the ability to travel without a Gate," mused Alephander. "A demon or an angel."

"Are there any Elf, Shifter or human wizards besides yourself who could do it?" asked Michael.

"If so, this person has concealed her ability from me," said Alephander. He sounded annoyed. "On Main Street in my own town, no less!"

"Finally, the fifth suspect," said Miles. "Is Raziel Renaci himself."

Chet shook his head. "Michael, how is that possible? I thought your people couldn't manifest Dark magic any more than mine could manifest Light."

"Maybe it happened after he defected..." suggested Moxie.

Michael shook his head. He looked uncomfortable. "Raziel has always had the ability to use Dark magic. Yes, it's rare, but not impossible for one born in Dayhaven. This isn't widely known, but Raziel is a Nemesis Angel. He has the ability to rip out a person's heart and control it."

"*Now* you tell us!" exclaimed Moxie.

"Alephander knew," said Michael defensively.

"Oh, of course *Alephander* knew!" Moxie stood and paced angrily.

"Did you know this, Chet?"

Chet shook his head. "At least when I was assigned to guard him, Raziel was careful to keep the details of his powers secret. Believe me, if we had known, we would have made him use that power."

"Are you saying he's still resisting complete cooperation with the demons?" asked Michael.

"When I knew him," said Chet carefully, "Which was several months ago, remember, he would obey a direct command, but he never volunteered anything. All of you assume that he didn't know that Miles wouldn't stay dead if Raziel killed him. Don't assume that. Raziel might have recognized that Miles was the Hanged Man... and not warned Glug'ulgros. Then again, although only months have passed for us, Raziel has spent years of repeated time being tortured in the Pit of Tartarus. Much more time has passed for him than most of us. His will may have been completely broken by now. Why else would he have bonded to a worm like Vass? Vass is a spoiled brat, and he was one of Raziel's torturers."

"It sounds like Stockholm Syndrome to me," said Kyrah.

"Whatever fancy name you give it, the demons recruit through too methods: pain and pleasure. They punish resistance and, at the same time, they also get their victims addicted to Dark magic. Even ordinary food in Darkpyre is addictive. It works. It's nearly impossible to break that conditioning."

Miles thought back to his interactions with Raziel. Had the dark angel given any indication he thought Miles would survive? Not really. Rather, Raziel seemed convinced, even envious, that Miles would die, and his spirit would move on to the Last Home.

"If Raziel was protecting someone he cared about," said Miles, "If he thought the only way he could do it was to slaughter every single Guardian, I think he would have had both the will power and the magic to do it."

Alephander drummed the table with his fingers. "I never considered him before. This changes things. We need to know when he switched sides." Alephander raised his eyebrows at Miles. "It looks like you have your work cut out for you, detective."

"What? Me?"

"The case isn't solved yet."

"I'll need a partner." Miles looked at Mercy. "I couldn't have got far without you."

She smiled shyly. No one would have guessed she had fought off hundreds of reapers, harpies, and demons single-handedly.

"We will all help," said the Emperor. "If you need muscle, apply to Victoria and me, and you'll have Knights and Dragons to aide you. If you need a more subtle form of strength, Moxie is your girl. If you need someone to hack a computer, ask Maverick Cade. If you need luck, ask Owen McGee. If you need lawfare, ask Eleni Bendox. We all work together as a team. That's the power of the Guardians. And there are more Guardians we've yet to find."

Epilogue

July 31, Sunday

ALTHOUGH JULY WAS AT AN END, every day of the month fireworks had gone off over Mystic Lake. It wasn't as bright a display as for the Fourth, but it still looked beautiful reflected against the water. Miles still couldn't believe the adorable house he had found on the market. With the money from his salary as well as for the job he had done for the Magician he had no trouble putting a down payment on a lakefront cottage. It wasn't huge, but it was big enough for him and his beautiful bride. They had married in a quiet ceremony that very morning.

As part of their human cover stories, Mercy continued to work as a nurse in the Veteran's Hospital, and Miles continued to hang his shingle as a private eye. Mercy asked Miles to help her keep an eye on the hospital, so evil-doers couldn't corrupt its mission of healing again. Miles asked Mercy to help him provide special services to his clients that he wouldn't have been able to do before.

For instance, when he met with Gini Brown to tell her that she was right, her boyfriend had been murdered, but the culprit had been caught and brought to justice, Mercy arrived. Gini apologized for thinking Mercy was a murderer. Mercy asked Gini if she wanted to speak to Gawain one last time.

Wide-eyed, Gini agreed.

The ghost of the centaur soldier had a private talk with his former girlfriend. Miles and Mercy didn't eavesdrop, but afterward, a tearful Gini said, "Thank you for allowing us to speak together one last time. He told me he wants me to find a new love, not to mourn him, he's in a great place."

However, although Mercy and Miles still had their separate jobs, they decided they would officially tie the knot and live together. Hence the cottage by the lake.

"You're not going to seriously try to lift me over the threshold, are you?" she asked.

"Are you suggesting you want to transform into your Valkyrie self and lift me? Because we all know you are strong enough."

"Do you want me to?" she asked. "I'm too fat in my human form, aren't I?"

"You have curves. That's not fat. And haven't I told you how strong I am?" He scooped her into his arms. She squealed and laughed as he threw her over his shoulder in a fireman's hold.

"Miles!" she chided. "Not upside down!"

"Oh, am I doing it wrong?" he grinned.

He jostled her and then scooped her up in his arms like a proper bride. He carried her across the threshold of their new house, then kissed her.

"Welcome to our new home, Mrs. Malone."

If you enjoyed this book...

Please write a review on the site where you bought it. Even a line or two helps indie authors like me continue to bring you more novels to enjoy.

You can also write to me if you would like to tell me which character in this novella you would like to know more about! Several characters who appeared here are certain they will never fall in love, but the Light may have other plans.... Whose story would you love to read?!

If you liked this book, you will also enjoy the other novels and novellas set in Arcana Glen. These are all stand-alone Happily-Ever-After romances set in the Arcana universe, with recurring characters and an ongoing alternate history. Each series has an interconnected overarching story, but still has its own Heroine and Hero and happy, complete ending. Each book, even within a series, can be read and enjoyed independently.

Next up in the Major Arcana series is ***The Demon & the Dryad***. As with all the Arcana Glen romances, ***The Demon & the Dryad*** is a complete love story, but related to the ongoing quest to find all the new

Guardians and the murderer who framed the Magician for the Massacre of the old Guardians.

Also check out ***The Sherif's Magic Summer Jail Break***, a holiday novella in the same universe. These shorter holiday-themed novellas in the Arcana Glen Cycle of the Year series can be read any time of year, just like any Arcana Glen novels.

Be sure and grab ***The Genie & the Gymnast***, a stand-alone Prequel sweet paranormal romance to The Major Arcana series.

Cast for Death & the Detective

HERO & HEROINE:

- **Miles Malone** – a human who was mundane until he suffered a near-death incident while on the police force. Unaware of the transformation, he left the police force and became a private investigator in Arcana Glen.
- **Mercy Wise** – a Valkyrie living in Arcana Glen, who works at the Arcane Veteran's hospital. Her human job is a nurse, but her arcane position is a reaper of the dead.

Staff and Patients at Arcana Glen Veteran's Hospital:

- ***Beverly "Bev" Howard*** – another nurse who is human and mundane.
- ***Dr Warren Winters*** – a physician.
- ***Dr Richard Sharpe*** – a physician.
- ***Dr Augustus Cornel*** – a highly renowned specialist physician.
- ***Braic O'Malley*** – a patient on the verge of death.
- ***Corey Ming*** – a patient who had his appendix removed.

- *Miguel Ramos* – a patient at Arcana Glen Veteran's Hospital; a Coyote Shifter
- *Henry Burnhard* – a patient at Arcana Glen Veteran's Hospital; a Bear Shifter.
- *Tony Ban* – a patient at Arcana Glen Veteran's Hospital; a mundane who was injured in a Dragon attack.

GUARDIANS WHO APPEAR IN THIS TALE:

- *Alephander Guiscard* - *The Magician*
- *Bethany Dilly Guiscard* - *The Fool*
- *Kyrah Nestor*- *The Seeress*
- *Sabriel Izbognir* – the previous Seeress before Kyrah; having been murdered, she is now a spirit.
- *Michael "Pastor Mike" Lamb* - *The Hierophant*

OTHERS WHO APPEAR IN THIS TALE:

- *Sheriff Cody Lawson* – a young, new sheriff who replaced his older brother, Spencer Lawson. A human mundane.
- *Gini Brown* – a client who comes to Miles Malone for help to prove that her boyfriend was murdered.
- *John Helwall* – a construction worker who runs the forest gym path with Miles.
- *Gawain Herle* – the boyfriend of Gigi Brown.
- *Hawke Mayers* – a Valhalla Warrior that Mercy's parents invite to dinner
- *Pamela Newton* – (not in the book, only mentioned) real estate agent
- *Lindsey Olsen* – (not in the book, only mentioned) a girl Miles once asked out
- *Eva White* – Miles Malone's secretary
- *Gulda Wise* – Mercy's mother
- *Maurice Wise* – Mercy's father
- *Maven Wise* – Mercy's sister

- ***Merlin Wise*** – Mercy's brother
- ***Sumiko Sadukatzu*** – a Shinigami reaper who is visiting from Japan.
- ***Xin Glug'ulgros*** – the Demon King of Gluttony
- ***Yorgath the Undying Scourge*** – Mercy's ex, a reaper, whose arcane shape is a 9' skeleton in a bloody clown suit.

- STRAT (Military Science Fiction)
- CIVIS (Strat Book 2 - Coming)

Books on Writing:

- 30 Day Novel: No Fail Formulas to Finish Your Novel

walk away or fight for her... assuming she would even accept the help of an exile.

$$\sim$$

"I was enchanted by Initiate, drawn into a world that felt as comfortably recognizable and uniquely untried as Narnia, Hogwarts or Middle Earth."

CASEE MARIE, THE GIRL WHO STOLE THE
EIFFEL TOWER

"Wow. Holy smoking wow. This is one of the few books I've read that I can honestly say was totally, 100% original.... However, as unique as it is, it was insanely easy to slip into the story..."

EMI LONDON, OCTOPUS INK

"I recommend this [series] ...to fantasy and epic saga lovers and readers who liked reading Lord of the Rings, but found the length of the book overwhelming....This book series has a unique concept - breaking down the traditionally long Epic Fantasy tale into shorter more manageable books."

GINA, MY PRECIOUS: RAMBLINGS OF A
KINDLE ADDICT

Start reading Initiate right now!

The Hot Dog Detective

BETRAYED BY HIS WIFE, *mocked by the man who murdered her, fired from the police department, MacFarland remakes himself as a hot dog vendor. But then a murder draws him back into the justice business...*

Betrayed by his wife and the system, former Denver Police Detective Mark MacFarland dropped out of the system...all the way. But now he has put drinking and homelessness behind him, bought a hot dog stand, and started a new life.

Then a noted defense lawyer asks MacFarland to prove that his client was wrongly accused of murdering her husband. Suddenly, MacFarland's past catches up with him.

· · ·

Aided by his former partner, Cynthia Pierson, and his longtime homeless friend, Vietnam Vet Rufus, MacFarland discovers the husband's murder is actually part of a larger web of conspiracy...and may even tie in to the death of his wife.

Read the first book in this "cozy noir" mystery series for free.

Click here to read.

www.ingramcontent.com/pod-product-compliance
Lightning Source LLC
Chambersburg PA
CBHW070811170726
48000CB00017B/260